FROM A ROOM OF THEIR OWN

THE KATHERINE MANSFIELD FELLOWS

1970	OWEN LEEMING
1971	MARGARET SCOTT
1972	C.K. STEAD
1973	JAMES McNEISH
1974	JANET FRAME
1975	DAVID MITCHELL
1976	MICHAEL KING
1977	BARRY MITCALFE
1978	SPIRO ZAVOS
1979	PHILIP TEMPLE
1980	MARILYN DUCKWORTH
1981	LAURIS EDMOND
1982	MICHAEL JACKSON
1983	ALLEN CURNOW
1984	ROWLEY HABIB
1985	MICHAEL GIFKINS
1986	MICHAEL HARLOW
1987	RUSSELL HALEY
1988	LOUIS JOHNSON
1989	LLOYD JONES
1990	LISA GREENWOOD
1991	NIGEL COX
1992	MAURICE GEE
1993	WITI IHIMAERA

From a Room of Their Own

A Celebration
of the
Katherine Mansfield
Fellowship

SELECTED AND INTRODUCED BY MICHAEL GIFKINS

PAINTINGS BY PETER FEATHERSTONE

Whitcoulls Limited
Auckland

David Ling Publishing Limited
Birkenhead, Auckland

From a Room of Their Own
First Edition

ISBN   0–908990–06–5

First published 1993

Introduction and this selection © Michael Gifkins 1993
Paintings © Peter Featherstone 1993
This edition © David Ling Publishing Limited 1993
Copyright in the individual contributions to this
book are listed on page 153

Design by Biggles & Co. and Julie Roil
Typeset by Egan-Reid Ltd
Printed in Hong Kong

CONTENTS

Brockie

Menton
Garavan
Isola Bella
3.IX.89

Introduction

Writing in 1977, the late Celia Manson (whose energies were the guiding force in the early years of the Fellowship which originally bore her name: the Winn-Manson Menton Trust) confirmed the chief purposes of what was then, and is still today, New Zealand's only overseas literary bursary of any consequence:

'It aims to give a selected New Zealand writer a period of leisure to write or study, to expose them to a different and more ancient culture, and thereby to allow them to see their own remote country in better perspective.

'It aims to help international relations by the fact of enabling a New Zealand writer to work each year in France.

'It aims by the same means to improve New Zealand's cultural image overseas.'

These aims are perhaps even more relevant today than they were then.

The Fellowship, and its incumbent at the time, have survived French nuclear testing in the Pacific and New Zealand protest at this, both through diplomatic channels and by the direct action (inconceivable today) of despatching a frigate into the testing zone. It has withstood the sinking of the Greenpeace vessel *Rainbow Warrior* in Auckland Harbour by frogmen of the DGSE—an act which still resonates through the corridors of power in France. And most recently, it has been unaffected by the protest of French farmers at threats to their livelihood from New Zealand imports. Throughout these periods of turbulence the Fellowship has flourished, even when diplomatic relations have virtually ceased. Some might argue that it has been able to continue unscathed because it has remained unnoticed, but the truth is more likely to lie in the French ability to divorce politics from matters of art. Literature (and writers) occupy a considerably more elevated position in their pantheon than they do in our own. In this small way, the pen has been seen to be mightier than the sword.

Nor have the Fellows at moments of political crisis been greatly affected personally. For a time, visas were required for travel from New Zealand to France. As anyone who has dealt with French bureaucracy will know, this posed more stumbling blocks than might initially have been apparent. But the real enemy for Fellows has always been not the government of France, nor even local body politicians in the form of the Mairie, the procedures of which, while always formal and often

Owen Leeming, the first Fellow, outside the Memorial Room in 1970. The brass plaque on the lefthand side of the doorway gives Katherine Mansfield's date and place of birth and death and quotes from a 1920 letter to Middleton Murry: 'You will find Isola Bella in pokerwork on my heart.' The righthand plaque lists the stories completed at Isola Bella, including 'Poison' and 'Daughters of the Late Colonel'.

(left) Bob Brockie's 1989 pencil drawing of Isola Bella. The Memorial Room is at the lower left of the building.

intimidating, are in all essential matters, as Nigel Cox reports, far more efficient than our own. The true battleground for international relations has been that quintessentially French institution, *la poste*, bizarre, incompetent and sullen to an extent far exceeding its New Zealand equivalent even after deregulation here, and referred to by James McNeish, in what I am sure was an uncharacteristically fevered outburst, as 'the most infuriating institution in the world'.

Perhaps once a year, Corsica appears to rise from the sea just off Menton. This mirage is the product of a temperature inversion which bends the rays of light between the island and the viewer, in reality some 150 km apart.

In 1985, with diplomatic relations at flashpoint, my only real difficulty in Menton was dealing with the sniggering post office clerks whose attentions were suddenly focussed on the address of my letters home. Their ability to demean a foreigner in front of an always lengthy queue was awesome and needed strong measures to overcome it. After several days' practice so that the words tripped easily from my tongue, I finally announced that they may be able to say what they liked, but that I felt sure that regulations did not permit the attaching of a bomb to my letter. It was a riposte that was appreciated by the waiting crowd and the matter was not mentioned again.

By that stage I was known in town as a writer and some small part of the *cachet* which we dream of in New Zealand but with which we are rarely rewarded had already attached itself to my presence. It is a generosity that is typically European to honour artists, as most Fellows have discovered to their amazement and delight. In a climate free of the demand for self-justification we can do and say the things which may be at odds with the grosser movements on an international stage.

Planning for the first award of the Fellowship came to fruition in 1969 at a meal at the Domaine de Fontvieille, an old Provençal *bastide*, or farmhouse, about five kilometres outside Aix-en-Provence. Under nut trees in the shade of the arches of a great stone aquaduct that brought water from the Durance River across the dry plains of Provence, poet

Owen Leeming was invited by Cecil and Celia Manson to become the first Fellow in the largely neglected Memorial Room of the Villa Isola Bella, where Katherine Mansfield had lived and worked, writing a handful of her best stories while struggling with the illness that was soon to kill her.

This was about the time that a man first landed on the moon and the prospect of a New Zealand writer being funded, however minimally, to live and work for a month or two in the South of France must have seemed perhaps even more unlikely. The writers' organisation PEN were initially unenthusiastic, feeling they could not give even moral support to such a 'flamboyantly impossible' idea. It all fell back on the Mansons, with their burning desire that their country's literary heritage be preserved not just in stone, but in the form of the living presence of other writers following in Katherine Mansfield's footsteps. In this they had the support of the New Zealand Women Writers' Society, who had already done much to honour Mansfield's memory. The Mayor of Menton was encouraging. And with the equal enthusiasms of the Queen Elizabeth II Arts Council (which they translated into a seeding grant of $1000) and of private citizens, notably Sheilah Winn, who dipped into their own pockets to promote something they believed in, the Fellowship was born.

Since that time many of this country's greatest—or to become so—writers have made an annual pilgrimage to the small stone room in the pleasant township that marks one end of the fabled Côte d'Azur. They include Commonwealth prizewinners Allen Curnow and Lauris Edmond, and eminent novelists Janet Frame and Maurice Gee. But perhaps more importantly they number in their ranks writers perceived to be at a mid-point in their careers, at a crossroads where promise is about to be converted to significant achievement. It is a desire expressed by Celia Manson in her guidelines for awarding of the Fellowship, that it should act as a catalyst for precisely this transformation. Even so, her words have not always been heeded by a selection committee that changes every year, but includes members of the Trust that administers the Fellowship (though its day-to-day running is now in the hands of the QEII Arts Council) and invited literati, sometimes Fellows from previous years. There may in fact be an essential contradiction in the Fellowship's guiding document in that it overlooks the very human impulse to favour with more honours those who are already illustrious. For the fact remains that it was initially conceived not as a reward for long service or the highest achievement, but as helping writers whose promise was still perhaps equal to their achievement, something of which I am sure Katherine Mansfield herself would have approved.

Corporate support for the Fellowship has always been hard to come by, perhaps because it has been difficult for executives with one eye on the bottom line to ascertain what might be the *quid pro quo*. There has been the additional problem, shared to some extent, it seems, by the public at large, of the Fellowship being perceived less as an opportunity to write

Michael King and the great Australian novelist and Nobel prizewinner, Patrick White, outside Isola Bella in 1976. The building had been considerably freshened since Owen Leeming's time. Patrick White took the (relatively) impoverished writer out to the finest meal he'd had in Europe—CER at its early best.

while experiencing another culture, and more as an expenses-paid junket to a favoured destination, a sort of Club Med holiday in the South of France. But the money available to each year's Fellow has until recently been minimal, and still is enough to pay only an airfare and insurance and permit of very basic living for anything between four months and twelve—depending on how lucky the Fellow is in finding accommodation, which the Fellowship does not supply.

Considering that Menton is the favoured destination throughout the three months of the summer season of what seems, especially in August, like half of Europe, and that prices are pitched accordingly, it is little short of a miracle that some Fellows have been able to eke out their stipend for as long as they have. The truth, I suspect, is that many subsidise themselves to stay there longer, a few Fellows spending perhaps twice what the Fellowship affords them. The financial assistance in recent years of Electricorp Marketing, the Fellowship's present sponsors, has gone a long way towards overcoming financial problems, but even so the amount awarded in any one year is exactly the same as is given by the QEII Arts Council for a Scholarship in Letters, which allows a senior writer to work fulltime *at home in New Zealand* for a similar period.

The marketplace in Bandol. The extensive paving which makes careful allowance for specimen trees is a feature of French towns.

The door on the first floor of Isola Bella from which Katherine Mansfield would emerge each morning to take the air.

While being in a foreign country and writing for any length of time is an experience of startling originality, as much of the work in this anthology will testify, there is no way on earth that it is a junket. Tales of hardship—of tears, of early departures, even of the breakdown of marriage relationships—are what one hears at first or second hand, or is able to read between the lines.

The Fellowship makes no allowance for partners or families—no additional money is provided if the Fellow wishes to be accompanied, and of course accommodation for more than one is proportionately more expensive—or disproportionately, when it is considered that a writer by her or himself may well be prepared to put up with hardships that a couple, or a family, would not wish to tolerate. Perhaps unsurprisingly, under half of the 24 Fellows to date have travelled to Menton alone. Others have gone with partners, or with whole families. Those who have travelled alone have invariably been able to stay longer—before the money runs out.

So which is the ideal condition—alone or accompanied? There are trade-offs both ways. Alone, a writer is perhaps better able to pursue his or her craft, essentially a solitary occupation, not brooking interruption. Writers are traditionally solitary animals—except when they wish for company, at which times they can become overwhelmingly gregarious (these of course are almost meaningless generalisations). One of the stipulations of the Fellowship is that the Memorial Room be used for writing, which in practice means that the Fellow leaves from whatever accommodation has been secured, to 'go to work' every morning. This is a familiar enough phenomenon, but when it involves leaving a partner alone by themselves, perhaps twiddling their thumbs, in a town where they have neither friends nor acquaintances (at least not initially) and have no projects of their own—and may not even have sufficient language to make themselves understood at the bakery—then the possibilities for tension are obvious. Children, it is true, can and do go to school: this is an experience in itself, and one which I have yet to see the child of a Fellow write about. But for adults, the days can be filled with loneliness and even resentment of a partner's growing tally of words, and perhaps too their greater prestige: in terms of social standing, a writer is one thing, the partner of a writer, another. Margareta Gee went to France in 1992 with her husband, 'the writer' (she refers to him as 'TW'), prepared for the worst contingencies. As a result, she appeared to survive very well: 'I come from a long line of women skilled at being happily occupied. This capacity for being busy, but not going round in circles or polishing the bathroom taps, stood me in good stead for life in Menton.'

Which leads to the twinned subjects of language acquisition, and of 'experience'. With regard to the former, it is probably easier to learn a language if you are forced to speak it every day, and have no familiar nest where English is spoken as a matter of course, to return to when the going

Poet David Mitchell receiving a presentation from the Mayor of Menton. In 1975 the new generation of New Zealand writers were almost uniformly longhaired and minimally garbed. In preparation for the Fellowship, David Mitchell had his hair cut and then, remembering the Frenchmen he'd seen in movies, bought the best leather jacket he could afford in Sydney on the way to France. The result had him looking like a Niçois gangster and left the bemused matrons at his reception muttering about 'le blouson noir'.

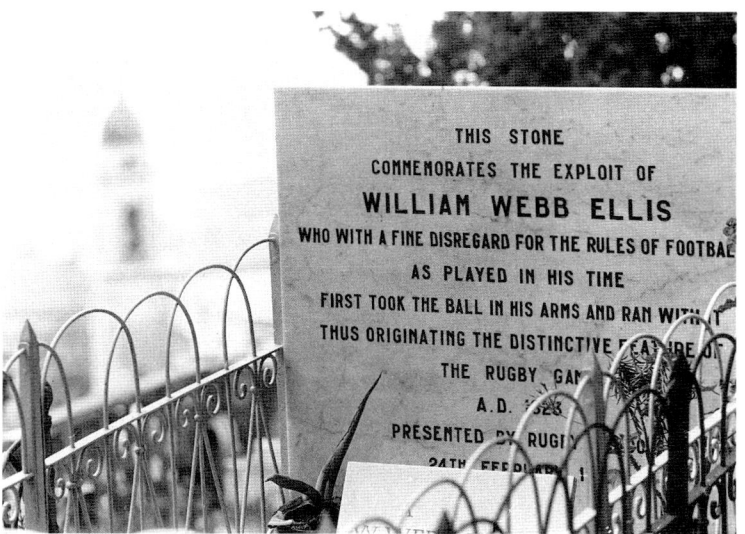

THIS STONE
COMMEMORATES THE EXPLOIT OF
WILLIAM WEBB ELLIS
WHO WITH A FINE DISREGARD FOR THE RULES OF FOOTBALL
AS PLAYED IN HIS TIME
FIRST TOOK THE BALL IN HIS ARMS AND RAN WITH IT
THUS ORIGINATING THE DISTINCTIVE FEATURE OF
THE RUGBY GAME
A.D. 1823
PRESENTED BY RUGBY SCHOOL

The tombstone in the Menton cemetery most likely to make a New Zealander feel at home.

gets tough. Rowley Habib is on record as saying that he did not speak to anyone at all, did not utter even a single word, *for weeks* after his arrival in Menton. At the supermarket, his only point of social contact, he was able to select what he wanted, pay, and leave without making a sound. As for 'experience', it is a truism that a single person is likely to receive more, and more interesting, invitations, and is more readily able to make each new experience their own, rather than a shared one: not in itself particularly desirable or even commendable, but for a writer, the very stuff of their work.

On the other hand, a stranger in a (relatively) strange land can take great comfort from returning home to one or more familiar faces or voices after each day's work. And it is equally true to say that to share something can be to double the pleasure. In the final analysis, no one situation would seem to be better. You are paid your money and you take your chances. My own suspicion, however, (and I am aware that it is merely a reflection of my experience), is that the writer travels furthest who travels alone.

James McNeish high above the Côte d'Azur in 1973.

The matter of language is often a stumbling block for Fellows, and there is no doubt that the more French one knows (and can actually use in day-to-day situations, not necessarily the same thing), the better equipped one is to make an unfamiliar setting seem less daunting. As is widely known, the French are sticklers for their language; they can talk like machineguns, using words and constructions that seem to bear no relationship to French as it is taught at secondary school in New Zealand. And unlike (say) the Italians, they are not usually indulgent and approving of foreigners whose attempts to communicate come out as dissonant manglings of their native tongue. Even so, it is better to try than not. And while it may be beyond any Fellow's reach to, say, discuss post-

structuralism with a Sorbonne academic (although I defy anyone to succeed in this, even in English) it can become, especially with some basic notions of the language already established before arrival, perfectly satisfying bullying waiters and especially taxidrivers (who often seem to require this treatment) in their own tongue, or chatting with the plumber, or with the elderly Niçoise who shares your *couchette* for the all-night train trip to Paris with her incontinent cat. It is interesting that Owen Leeming, the Fellow who never went home, now works as a translator (from French into English) with the OECD in Paris.

There is a broader issue to consider here, and that is not so much who is awarded Fellowships, but who actually applies for them. Because the Fellowship is rigorous in its demands—the Fellow must leave the country, and their job if they have one apart from writing; and may also have to leave a partner, or a young family, if circumstances dictate this— I suspect that some fine writers are discouraged from even applying. In the present climate, how easy might it be to be granted a year's leave-of-absence from a job? How is it possible to leave a hefty mortgage? How easy is it to travel with a baby? Would one want to *leave* a baby with one's partner?

Isola Bella with the Memorial Room, reputed to be the wine cellar (or the toolroom) in Katherine Mansfield's time, at the bottom left. The incumbent Fellow does not have access to the rest of the Villa, but is never at a loss for company with trains going past the Room every 15 minutes in the summer. The platform for passengers bound for Italy is at the bottom of the picture.

This is not a judgment on either these writers or the Fellowship. It is a point worth making, though, that there are sacrifices either way: in not applying, and so possibly missing out on the experience; or in applying, and knowing that large compromises may be necessary if the application is successful.

Finally there is the consideration that France, *per se*, might not be everyone's cup of *thé*. This is perfectly understandable. Some people do not want to leave home, ever, and neither their lives, nor their writing (if they are writers) are necessarily impoverished as a result. Even the Côte d'Azur as a destination turns off as many people as it excites. Some New Zealanders prefer the Gold Coast, others Disneyland. For many, London is the ultimate destination. It does not devalue these preferences to say quite simply that Menton is to the Fellowship as Menton was to Katherine Mansfield: the place where she wrote. The Memorial Room could equally well be located in Bandol (which has its own virtues), where she also stayed. But it's not. And that is precisely the point.

A view of the old town of Menton from Garavan in 1973. The fishing port is on the left and the spire of the Eglise St Michel rises above the town.

The Fellows, as a whole, are an adventurous lot. But even if they are used to taking risks in their writing—used to pushing back the boundaries of what it is possible to say, and how it is possible to say it— it is not without trepidation that they leave on the 20,000 kilometre journey to the South of France. Many have never before been out of New Zealand. In spite of speaking to past Fellows, no one knows exactly how it will be for them. Will they be able to survive? Will they even be able to *write*?

Which leads me to a final issue. It has been fashionable in certain quarters over the past few years to decry the need, or even the possibility of the need, in a writer that makes him or her want to be in an environment other than their natural one (New Zealand), or to look for inspiration beyond these shores. Carried to an extreme, this position reveals its own absurdity: how, one might ask, would this country have been settled had not first the Maori and then European explorers felt the need to discover what was here? It is the same with writing. The experience of Menton is much more, as Celia Manson knew, than having free time in which to write. It is an experience of another culture in another place; but more importantly it is the experience of oneself in relation to these things, the writer's charting of inner responses and personal resonances, the ultimate value of which, and its ultimate interest to others, the contributions to this anthology may help establish.

The grandson of Katherine Mansfield's landlady at the Villa Pauline in Bandol. He died a few weeks after this photo was taken.

It is perhaps unsurprising that writers well acquainted with shorelines of great natural beauty should want to write about a coast that is redolent of the movements of history and resonates with innuendoes of both its actual and its literary past. Many of the writers included here (especially the poets) have captured aspects of the Côte d'Azur while actually working at the Villa Isola Bella. Others recall it in the poignancy of its absence. In selecting material for inclusion in this book, commemorative of the Katherine Mansfield Memorial Fellowship's 25th anniversary, I have restricted myself to three areas of past (and present) Fellows' writing: either material written about the Menton experience while resident there; or material which recalls it, written while resident somewhere else (most usually New Zealand); or a final category, comprising writing done during the tenure of the Fellowship, but which in no way refers to it (Maurice Gee's extract fits here, as does Witi Ihimaera's). This last group of pieces is interesting in the degree to which the experience of being abroad serves to highlight in the mind's eye the environment which the writer has most recently left behind (a kind of creativity through homesickness, if you like). In the case of Spiro Zavos, his Wellington material seemed to him unusually heightened in Menton, even glowing, and suddenly begged to be explored.

The thing most interesting about Menton, apart from the fact of Katherine Mansfield's staying there, is that it is part of the Côte d'Azur, or the French Riviera, which in many essential ways has far less to do with France than it has to do with the people and the fashions that have 'created' it over the past 150 years.

It was originally an impoverished sea-coast hinterland, dotted with fishing villages isolated one from the other and having little to do with the national life of France. Now, through being colonised by writers, artists, gamblers, expatriates and affluent holidaymakers of many nationalities, but especially English, American and Russian, all looking for a place

NOUVELLE-ZELANDE - MENTON

PALAIS DE L'EUROPE

ANNIVERSAIRE DES 10 ANS D'ASSOCIATION ENTRE LA
NOUVELLE-ZÉLANDE ET MENTON
PAR LA FONDATION DE L'ÉCRIVAIN KATHERINE MANSFIELD

EXPOSITION

26 Novembre · 15 Décembre 1979

PHILIP TEMPLE, Boursier de la Fondation Katherine Mansfield 79

présente

GENS ET SITES

Photographies de l'Ile du Sud de la Nouvelle-Zélande

CINEMA

Mercredi 28 Novembre 1979 à 16 h.

Présentation spéciale de Films Documentaires sur
la NOUVELLE-ZÉLANDE (en Version Française)

ENTRÉE GRATUITE pour les deux manifestations

Imp. Ciquet - Menton

The handbill for Philip Temple's photographic exhibition and screening of New Zealand films— shockingly green pastures, fabulous scenery and thousands of sheep.

where they could become real to themselves as the subjects of their dreams, the Riviera has become part mega-industry, part myth, beloved especially by those escaping from the mundanity of the everyday and of their identity as people anywhere else might perceive it. As a geographical location it has no *essential* reason for being as it now is. And equally, the Côte d'Azur exists too as a country of the mind where the rules are not quite the same as obtain in other places. Mary Blume's recently published book, *Côte d'Azur: Inventing the French Riviera* (Thames and Hudson, 1992) is particularly good at explaining this.

This is why it is beloved by criminals, who haunt the casinos and are believed to have been responsible for the death (read murder) of Princess Grace of Monaco. Nor is it an accident that the film industry's greatest event occurs annually not in Hollywood, but just along the coast from Menton, at Cannes. It is also the reason that the Côte d'Azur is haunted by writers, and why so many of them live there. Other Fellows will understand that I am not boasting when I say that in one day I had lunch with Graham Greene in Antibes, bumped trolleys with Anthony Burgess in a supermarket in Monte Carlo (his was full of catfood), and that night met Shirley Conran at a party in Cap d'Ail.

The reason so many writers gravitate towards the Côte d'Azur (and earlier figures such as Scott Fitzgerald also spring to mind) is twofold: on the one hand, they can follow their craft without let or hindrance (if indeed they can afford to be there); and on the other, they can make up glorious lies. While everyone around them is recreating themselves in their own best images, what better to do than to record this? Or, partaking of the quasi-divine madness, tell the stories that at home one might never have dreamed to tell.

A little of this creeps into the present anthology: perhaps mainly as an excitement at the *difference* of the place, a feeling that anything goes. It sits in a complex and appealing way in Lloyd Jones' account of an American writer satisfying only the dreams of supermarket booksellers and of his agent, while he (Lloyd Jones) has eyes only for the ghost of notorious payroll robber George Wilder, who materialises at every turn.

The medieval village of Eze, viewed from the McNeish's hilltop.

More obviously, it occurs in a generalised tendency among the writers represented here to mythologise the place: in this case, Menton and its environs. There is Corsica, rising from the sea through a trick of the light—a relatively rare phenomenon, but which every Fellow appears to have seen and noted. It occurs in the number of times the *clochard* appears in prose and verse: there can only be one beggar for Katherine Mansfield Fellows, and it is every time the professor (or 'the preacher'). He is the subject of Rowley Habib's poem, and Michael Jackson's novel extract is devoted to him; in a story of Marilyn Duckworth's not included here (the title piece in her volume *Explosions on the Sun*), he saves the narrator from being raped; he has a role in my own recently published story, 'Grimaldi Man'. It is fascinating to follow a character who appears in real life to have emerged from fiction, as he is recreated in other fictions as they appear on the printed page.

Beyond this, the Katherine Mansfield Fellowship, and the environs of the Memorial Room, are revealed more as a tiny principality—a New Zealand possession on the Riviera—whose intensity through being 'imagined' by its writers is no less (and because it is becoming so well documented, possibly even greater) than that other synthetic eminence, the Principality of Monaco. There are its boundaries—of the village of St Agnès in the foothills of the Alpes Maritimes, and Ventimiglia, just past the Italian border, and of Monte Carlo, a few kilometres the other way. There are the landmarks of the Eglise St-Michel, and the monastery of the Annonciade—to say nothing of the Mairie, the modern-day inquisitor's chamber. There are the identities—such as the expatriate writer, the late Anton Vogt, imagined (created? recreated?) equally vividly, but very differently, by Michael King, and by Lauris Edmond. Part of the pleasure of reading this anthology, and then of going further to the source works from which extracts are taken, will be (or so I hope and imagine) to track down the different influences from which the Fellows create this new reality, and of the different uses to which they put what are essentially the same raw materials.

And like all principalities, that of the Katherine Mansfield Fellowship has its own myths which run parallel to those created on paper by its writers—in fact, concern them more directly in that they are told by and about themselves. There is the myth (by the word I mean only a true story that has passed into legend) of the Fellow who infuriated the Mairie by regularly drying his smalls on the bushes in the Memorial Room's garden, to the great surprise of serious-minded Japanese and German students of literature visiting this almost-holy shrine. Or of the Fellow who went alone to France and came back to New Zealand with his Menton landlady. Or my favourite, which concerns the poet David Mitchell, who when invited to a special audience in Monaco with Prince Rainier and Princess Grace, completely forgot the 5.30 appointment because he had found an acolyte on the beach in the form of a lovely schoolgirl escaping

William Waterfield Esq, of the Clos du Peyronnet in Garavan. Mentor to grateful Fellows from Marilyn Duckworth (1980) on, William disproves most of the stereotypes about the English on the Côte d'Azur, encapsulating those that remain in benign and charming form.

The renowned *clochard* as remembered by a decade of Fellows in poetry and prose (see especially Michael Jackson's piece, and Rowley Habib's poem). Once a year the Menton gendarmes take him in and allow him the use of their washing facilities, then provide him with a new set of clothes—a sort of safety net of social security, proving that these can be slung just as low as ruling powers like.

This photo was taken in 1985. In 1993 he apparently looks much the same, and will probably continue to do so as long as there are KM Fellows in Menton. The reason the one-time maths teacher is so memorable for writers is possibly his air of complete self-sufficiency, and the way in which his isolation is symbolic of their condition—or at least when they are writing.

for eight days from Paris and the rigours of preparing for her baccalauréat. (When David Mitchell had asked in advance what sort of poems their Highnesses would like to hear, he had been told they would rather like to be entertained by 'something which made them smile'). And finally, slightly larger than life and creator of many of his own myths, there is expatriate Englishman William Waterfield, Eton and Oxford educated and inheritor of a family mansion in Garavan not five minutes from the Memorial Room: friend, devil's advocate and gruff mentor to a decade of Fellows, William occurs here in Lauris Edmond's diary extract, though elsewhere he crops up frequently, and in my own writing as well.

The writer of this introduction nursing a small gin on Dorothy Martin's *terrasse* in the Palais Ausonia in 1985. The *Rainbow Warrior* was sunk in Auckland Harbour the next day.

This, then, is Katherine Mansfield's territory, now colonised and reshaped in their own image by those writers who have been fortunate enough to hold the Fellowship that bears her name. It remains only to thank the Fellows who have readily given assent to and assistance with this anthology, and to thank too David Ling, whose good idea it was. Peter Featherstone has travelled several times to the south of France to paint, both with fellow artists and *en famille*. His paintings are another, parallel recreation of the myth of the French Riviera and sit easily with the written contributions. Julie Roil's assistance with the design of the book helps combine the exuberance and the elegance which characterise the writing and are also features of the Côte d'Azur lifestyle. James and especially Helen McNeish, many of whose photographs I have used, were instrumental in adding this extra dimension to the book, as was their friend David Playne, who printed at short notice for me from negatives held in England. Less directly, at the beginning of this, the twenty-fifth year of the Fellowship, I would like to thank past and present members of the Katherine Mansfield Memorial Trust, and the Mayors, past and present, of the City of Menton, who jointly sustain the Memorial which this book commemorates, both by honouring Katherine Mansfield and by celebrating the road down which other writers now travel.

Michael Gifkins
Auckland, New Zealand
1993

MICHAEL KING

*Michael King (b.1945) is a distinguished historian who has written
extensively on Maori and wider New Zealand history. He is the
author of more than twenty books and has won awards for literature
(including the Goodman Fielder Wattie Award for his 1989 title
Moriori: A People Rediscovered), television writing and journalism.
In 1988 he received the OBE for services to New Zealand history.*

A Patriot Abroad

To reach Menton and the Katherine Mansfield Fellowship I made my way by car down the eastern side of France—through the Somme, Amiens, Ardennes, Reims, Verdun, the great battlefields of the First World War. It was an awesome experience: miles of graves (one of them my paternal grandfather's), new towns built on the sites of ancient ones entirely laid waste, medieval buildings left mutilated, local museums filled with photographs and medals and mud-caked relics of war dug up on their doorsteps. Witnessing the scale of destruction and loss of life, and feeling the still palpable sense of death that pervades that part of the country, it was easier to understand why some Frenchmen chose to capitulate in World War Two.

I descended through Dijon, Lyon, the Rhone Valley, and burst finally into Provence, a stark and beautiful landscape: tree-crowded towns, Roman ruins, medieval villages. And everywhere the smell of lavender, thyme and Provençal cooking. Menton itself, on the French-Italian border, was a joy. It had an old town on the hill, dating from the thirteenth century and dominated by a baroque cathedral, St Michel. It had been the original home of the Grimaldis of Monte Carlo. Surrounding the old quarter was the new resort, sprawling along the shore of the Mediterranean.

Katherine Mansfield is New Zealand's major link with Menton and with France. She worked there in 1920, staying mainly at the villa Isola Bella with her companion Ida Baker. There she completed 'Daughters of the Late Colonel', 'The Young Girl', 'The Stranger', 'The Lady's Maid', and 'Poison', and she began a number of other stories. It was to commemorate this association that the Katherine Mansfield Fellowship was established in 1969. Garavan, where Isola Bella and the Katherine Mansfield fellow's writing room stand among stately homes and lush vegetation, is right on the Italian border, a mile east of Menton's old town. The Romans called Garavan the Bay of Peace and it still deserves that description. It is sheltered from prevailing winds and basks in sunshine for most of the year. It is a benign place in which to live and work.

I found the French (or at least the Mentonnais) polite and helpful, once they found that I was making serious efforts to speak their language and that I was the Boursier Katherine Mansfield. Some of their attitudes were in marked contrast to those back home. The words they used with most respect in conversation, for example, were écrivain, artiste, musicien—these were invested with the same reverence that New Zealanders reserve for 'doctor', 'lawyer', and 'accountant'. Specific highlights of the year were the music festival (which featured Richter and Michelangeli) and the town's art exhibition. The gardener in the villa at which I stayed had left school at the age of eleven; but in old age he recited poetry for hours at a time as he worked.

The district reeked of antiquity. It was there in the hard, shaped stone, in buildings that had contained human activity for centuries, in land that had been cultivated for millenia. The Via Aurelia, built by Julius Caesar to march his troops to Gaul and Britain, ran alongside the Katherine Mansfield Room; Roman monuments lie scattered along the coast, most of them in better condition than those in Italy. And internationalism is unavoidable. On one memorable day I had breakfast in France, lunch in Monte Carlo, and dinner in Italy—all without travelling more than five miles. All this impresses the sensitive colonial and triggers sometimes conflicting emotions.

It was helpful, though, to establish that one was not English. The antecedents of the English community in Menton go back to Queen Victoria (for whom the railway station next to the Katherine Mansfield Room was especially built) and to William Webb Ellis, the founder of rugby football, who is buried there close to Aubrey Beardsley. Both had gone there to recover from illness. The contemporary Menton-English lived like characters out of Somerset Maugham (who, after all, had lived only a few miles along the coast at Cap Ferrat). They had the exaggerated national characteristics of expatriates. Their lives were dominated by bacon and egg breakfasts, elevenses, gins and tonic, and a widespread unwillingness to speak French. They tolerated France, they told me, because of the climate and the absence of taxation. They were also the most snobbish and bitchy people I have encountered. Most defined themselves by whom they were related to or descended from (the *sister* of Michael Redgrave, the *mother* of Simon Gray); and in conversation they ran one another down ('He's put it around that she's been presented at Court. But my dear, she *hasn't*. She only met the Queen at a public function').

Aware of all this, I tended to exaggerate my non-English background. Once when I was buying liver, then changed my mind because of the price, the exasperated woman serving me threw up her arms and said, 'Ooo! Les Anglais!' 'Madame!' I said firmly. 'Je ne suis pas Anglais. Je suis Néo-Zélandais.' That didn't seem sufficient, so I continued. 'Mon grand-père est mort en France pendant la Grande Guerre. Pour votre patrie.' I didn't say that he had come from Scotland to die, not New Zealand. But the effect was startling. The woman put down the liver and wiped her fingers. She shook hands with me vigorously then went out the back to fetch her husband and three sons, who also shook hands with me. All the while the woman was saying, 'Son grand-père. Mort pour nous. . . .'

Given the freedom to go to a desk every day and simply write, without the need to earn supporting income, I finished the biography of Te Puea at Menton and began that of Andreas Reischek, the Austrian naturalist. I wrote more intensively than at any other time, before or since. And when the time came to leave, there were two climaxes that made the end of my stay as memorable as my arrival.

On my last night, I cleaned the floor of the Katherine Mansfield Room and left a present and a note for the incoming fellow, Barry Mitcalfe. Then I took a fond and final look and turned to leave. The door, however, would not open; the bolt had become detached from the handle. I opened the windows and experimented with easing myself through the bars on the outside. But I would have had to have been a three-stone midget to succeed. So I did something I had never had to do before in France: I called for help. 'Au secours, au secours!' It sounded oddly pedantic, not the least urgent; indeed, all I succeeded in doing was setting off a chain of barking dogs. Nobody came. Only once in the next two hours did a man walk past the room. I bellowed at him, but his passage coincided with that of the only goods train to go past, a long one, and he didn't hear a thing. In the end I had to attack the lock with a knife, a bottle opener and the heavy door handle, which I had managed to unscrew. I wrecked it completely and in the process got it off the door. And then I was able to escape. It was as if, as Anton Vogt told me romantically, the spirit of Mansfield was trying to detain me. If so, it was the only time she had made her presence known to me.

The finale was Corsica. Once a year Corsica shows itself to Menton, rising out of the sea like the Kaikouras from Island Bay. Only more jagged, more wild-looking—an untamed land facing a tamed one. The island was there the morning I left and it seemed auspicious: a rare occurrence to end a rare experience, like some kind of blessing. As I flew out of Nice on a mid-December afternoon, people were swimming. I found to my surprise that I was looking forward to London's crispness, its cold and snow. I had enjoyed six months of almost unrelieved sunshine and bright light. But, at the end, the Midi seemed characterised by a blandness I did not want to perpetuate. Mankind, Auden said, needs a gap. I certainly needed a gap. I was ready to return to the real world of seasons.

In the course of time in England, France, Germany and Austria, I had several opportunities to meet other writers. Some were immensely supportive: the New Zealand expatriates Dan Davin in Oxford, Kevin Ireland in London, and Anton Vogt in Menton, for example; Patrick White (who turned up in France as a tourist), Iris Murdoch, Arthur Koestler, Stephen Spender, Robert Lowell, John Betjeman and Nigel Nicholson.

I had heard of Anton Vogt—poet, teacher, performer—long before I left New Zealand. But I had never met him. He had emigrated in the early 1960s, releasing a stream of invective against the country's xenophobia, welfare-state mentality and inability (then) to tolerate diversity and eccentricity; especially its inability to tolerate Anton Vogt, who was colourful, clever and exuberant. I saw him first on Bastille Day 1976 on the balcony of a crowded restaurant on the French-Italian border. I watched in astonishment as an enthusiastic man got to his feet and entertained uncomprehending patrons with Rex Fairburn's parody of Michael Joseph Savage, *The Sky is a Limpet*. He had a fine voice for recitation, basso profundo, and was unperturbed by the confusion of his audience. The New Zealanders at his table were helpless with laughter, however, and I soon joined them. He encored with telling imitations of James K. Baxter and Denis Glover.

In the long friendship that followed, Vogt reminded me constantly that the eighteenth-century definition of patriotism had been that of a discontented man. A patriot, he said, is one who criticises his country unmercifully at home and defends it with equal intensity abroad. And this was precisely how he lived. In 1951, during Parliamentary Select Committee hearings on the Police Offences Act, the chairman, Clifton Webb, asked coldly: 'Mr Vogt, you're not a New Zealander, are you?' (Vogt had been born in Norway.) 'Mr Chairman,' Vogt replied, 'I am the only person in this room who is a New Zealander by choice.' And so he was.

The Night Streets of Arles
1992

Dan Davin, by contrast, was a donnish character who seemed to exemplify the dangers of leaving home too early, before establishing roots of one's own (as many of my own contemporaries had done). Son of a Southland railway worker, he went to Oxford on a Rhodes' Scholarship in 1935 and stayed there, completing an impressive career by becoming Academic Publisher for Oxford University Press. 'I am not a strong nationalist of any sort,' he told me. 'An expatriate by definition is an expatriate wherever he is. It doesn't matter where you live. You can't escape your dreadful self. And you'll always remember some other damned place that seems better than the one you're in.' Both Davin and Vogt, like Kevin Ireland, were generous and hospitable men who provided homes abroad for New Zealanders, emotional filling stations where travellers could re-charge themselves before moving on.

Of the other writers, my favourite was Iris Murdoch. She too had a New Zealand connection (her father was born there). At the PEN Congress in London, she showed a remarkable capacity to reduce complex matters to proportions that could be coped with in motions and resolutions. In conversation she exhibited a sense of mischievousness that seemed surprising in the light of the Gothic character of so many of her novels. She denied that, as her friend Davin alleged, her characters were unreal. 'Nonsense,' she said. 'People in life are all far more odd and sinister than they are in my fiction. But we often don't know this, because they are also secretive and cunning.'

It was confidence-building to meet people whom—from New Zealand—one could only admire at a distance; to talk with them, and to discover that they were human and in many cases displayed areas of ignorance and prejudice as large as those of anybody else. In general, though, the English delegates to the PEN Congress were patronising and distant, feeling no fellowship with writers of whom they had not already heard. And the Europeans acted like a closed club for their own amusement. Whereas the Americans there had huge appetites for encounters with new people and told their own life stories within five minutes. I can remember thinking it was a pity there could not be some kind of compromise among English reticence, Continental snobbishness, and American energy.

MARGARET SCOTT

Margaret Scott (b.1928) was the second Katherine Mansfield Fellow in Menton. She is editor, with Vincent O'Sullivan, of The Collected Letters of Katherine Mansfield and is currently preparing for press a four-volume edition of The Katherine Mansfield Notebooks.

123 Rue Longue

After an ill-omened arrival in Menton on April Fool's Day I had difficulty finding adequate accommodation, and several false starts at the hands of an estate agent disheartened me until he managed to come up with a room in the Old Town, in the beautiful, evocative and ancient rue Longue. One entered the building through a big old stone portico to find stairs up and stairs down. At the bottom of the flight going down was a small walled stone courtyard open to the sky. In the wall opposite the stairs were two doors of which one—mine—led into a large light room with a double window overlooking the sea and the hills of Italy.

The room had a double bed, a single bed, a card table and two chairs and an uncomfortable armchair. Off the room was a small kitchenette with fridge, gas stove and sink. Through another door off the main room was a tiny bathroom. In many ways I was lucky to have this accommodation in that it was central, sunny and roomy enough to enable me to entertain the stray New Zealanders and other ghosts from the past who drifted that way. Also it was very close to a small pebbly beach from which one could swim without having to pay—an important amenity for a New Zealander, though the oil-flecked warm water of that corner of the Med (hard by Le Vieux Port) scarcely evoked the cold green-and-white crashings on the shores of home. Its disadvantages were that its chattels were minimal and its rent was really more than I could afford—I had to borrow money to see me through.

At the top of the flight of stairs leading down to the little courtyard were two letter-boxes—one was mine and the other bore the legend 'Lorenzi Paul. Peintre.' This was clearly the name of the person in the apartment next to mine—and he was a painter! But of course—what more likely place to find a painter than in the South of France? He emerged proprietorially while I was moving in—a thin, elderly man with long restless limbs like an agitated insect. He hopped around offering advice, imparting information and asking questions in a kind of French that bore no audible relation to the French that 'Madame' taught me at school. It was clear, though, that he was full of goodwill and for this I had cause to be immediately grateful.

The first thing I discovered about my new apartment—before I had even unpacked—was that the lavatory was blocked. Luckily—my Harrap's English/French being still beyond reach—I remembered that a plumber was un plombier and I went next door to ask M. Paul (as

I called him) if he knew of one. He gave me a long stream of unintelligible information and then dashed up the stairs and came back in about one minute with a young man who proceeded expeditiously to unblock the lavatory. For this I was not charged.

There was nowhere in my apartment to work. The representative of the Department of Tourism, whose burden I was, told me variously that the 'Room' was unavailable, locked up, boarded up, unsuitable, unequipped, damp, unsafe. He assured me that no one came to the French Riviera to *work*. He patted me on the shoulder, smiled avuncularly and told me to run away and have fun. The sheer effrontery of this knocked the stuffing out of me for a while but I continued to importune them with my need for somewhere to work, and eventually, exasperated, they found a good big solid table and had it delivered to my address. M. Paul observed this with intense interest and evident curiosity. A day or two later he knocked on my door in the middle of the day and appeared to be inviting me to join him for lunch. I was alarmed. What lay behind this? What would my acceptance signify? In any case I was in the middle of something I didn't want to stop doing. I thanked him but declined, pleading busyness and indicating my big table full of folders of photocopies of Mansfield manuscript letters. He seemed to accept this with sympathy and understanding and scuttled away. A few minutes later he reappeared carrying a tray with my lunch on it: fried fish on one plate, meat balls in beans and tomato sauce with potato on another, a piece of lemon, a piece of cheese, a loaf of bread, an apple, une demi-bouteille de vin rouge. Ashamed of myself by then, I insisted that he bring his own to eat with me. Back he went, reappeared with his still in saucepans, tipped mine back into the saucepans, put them all on my gas rings turned low, and produced a bottle of marsala pour un apéritif. Later, when we had served up the meal he suddenly remembered he would need his teeth and dashed home again for those. We 'talked' for a couple of hours and, considering he had not a word of English and my small store of schoolgirl French was different from his, we managed wonderfully well. I had recourse to my Harrap's often enough but most of his chatter just flowed past me, occasionally brushing me with a familiar word. I found that his last painting job before he retired had been the Town Hall, and that his wife had died two years ago and he was lonely without her. He talked at great length about what happened in the war and I very much wished I could understand him because Menton is so close to the Italian border that it was difficult to imagine what it must have been like to live there during those times.

Certainly his war was exceedingly dramatic, his account of it punctuated with leapings up and down, detonations, bursts of carefully aimed machine-gun fire. At one point he shouted, 'Schweinhund!!'

'Schweinhund!' I shouted back—'I know what that word means.' This pleased him inordinately, apparently suggesting that I understood what he had been talking about. He jumped up, ran to the door of the apartment, beckoned me over and pointed to the walls of the little courtyard outside—walls which I could now see were pockmarked with bullet holes.

And somehow, through my lame and poverty-stricken French, he ascertained the essentials about me—Néo-Zélandaise, veuve, trois enfants, here for six or seven months to work, Fellowship, Katherine Mansfield's letters. Of course he had never heard of Kathérine Mansfield so we did not need to mention her again. My addressing him as M. Paul seemed to amuse him and he responded, still amused, by addressing me as Mme Margaret (presumably the postman had supplied the requisite information). When I began to receive mail from the French bank addressed to Mme Scott Margaret I suddenly realised that Lorenzi was his surname, Paul his given name. By that time I was somewhat embroiled. He had done me many small kindnesses and I was grateful to him. But he had written a totally unrealistic plot for this piece of fiction in which I, willy-nilly, had been assigned a main part. I was pretty sure quite early on that his intentions were, alas, honourable, but I couldn't see, within the parameters of ordinary civilised behaviour, how to blight them.

In the meantime other things were going on in my life, other people coming and going (though no other Mentonnais), and he, mon beau, who missed nothing except the significance of what he saw, tried to keep track of it all. There was quite a long period when he seemed to be trying to persuade me to go with him to Ventimiglia on the train one Saturday. He was very enthusiastic about how much I would enjoy it. I went to Ventimiglia a couple of times by myself but never did discover what might have been revealed if I had gone with him. Perhaps 'Saturday' was a euphemism for 'weekend'—perhaps *that's* what I missed! One afternoon, when I was coming down the stairs with a bag of groceries he darted out from his door excitedly telling me something about his television. 'En Anglais! En Anglais!' he said, pulling me by the arm into his darkened apartment. There on the television screen was Laurence Olivier. For a second I was afraid he might be about to embark on one of the francophobic speeches of *Henry the Fifth*, but no, he was Mr Darcy, dallying in a garden with Miss Elizabeth Bennet. I explained to M. Lorenzi that I had already seen it. Déjà vu.

He came in one afternoon for a drink (bringing with him a bottle of pastis and a bottle of grenadine). We had barely sat down when there was a knock at the door and I opened it to his sister whom I had met before and who lived just along the street. She was a solid, hard-headed, middle-aged French matron who spoke better French than he did and was easier to understand. She joined us in a drink sitting round the little table and proceeded to subject me to an inquisition. How long had I been a widow? Husband's profession? Cause of death? Number of children? Ages? State of health? She didn't ask what must have been the crucial question—whether I was worth anything. If there were things about me that made her dubious they were swept into insignificance when she observed on the table an invitation from the Mayor of Menton to be his guest at a concert of my choice during the Music Festival. This *profoundly* impressed her and with many nods and becks and wreathed smiles she explicated it to her brother and, I feel sure, gave him the go-ahead on the strength of it. (For the record, I should say that I naively thought that invitation meant that I would be joining the Mayor's party at the concert so I splashed out on a Paris gown. In the event, neither the Mayor nor any representative of his office appeared, and an usher told me to sit anywhere in the two back rows.)

While M. Lorenzi was fine-tuning his fantasy I was struggling with a host of other complex situations. We had frequent misunderstandings, inevitably. On one occasion he seemed to think I had agreed to walk out with him on a Sunday afternoon. I shudder to think of the probable significance in that small town of walking out together on a Sunday afternoon— I would certainly not have accepted an invitation to do so. But he turned up one dreadfully hot August afternoon dressed in a brand new pearl-grey suit and a simply splendid wide-brimmed pearl-grey hat—a sort of Al Capone outfit. I had to try to explain that I had misunderstood him and could not go out with him that afternoon. We were both so dismayed that I think that was the nadir of my interaction with him. The role I had been cast in was ludicrous, grotesque.

Quite soon after that he asked me to marry him. At least I think he did. No problem about the children, he said, they could all come to Menton to live with us. I tried to explain that there

The Tea Party
1991

were factors he knew nothing about. 'Pas possible?' he said, helpfully putting words in my mouth. 'Pas possible,' I said. His natural ebullience, however, was undiminished. In the morning I found hanging from my door-knob a paper bag containing two pears, a peach, a bread roll, and a strip of cardboard on which was pencilled 'Bonjour. Lorenzi'.

When I left Menton he stood out on the street and waved until the taxi turned the corner—the only real friend I made in all my seven months in that town. Back there ten years later I looked for him but all trace of him had gone.

Wellington, 1992

C.K. STEAD

C.K. Stead (b.1932) is an acclaimed novelist, poet, and literary critic who has received many awards for both his poetry and his fiction and was granted a CBE for services to New Zealand literature in 1985. His classic study The New Poetic: Yeats to Eliot *has been recommended reading in courses in 20th century English literature throughout the world for almost three decades. His most recent novel is* The End of the Century at the End of the World.

Buying a Car

I remember the first time I walked up into the hills behind the town and down to Garavan. I hadn't bought a car then—that's how I came to be on foot. I was looking for an apartment and there was one offering at Garavan. I'd walked there around the waterfront a couple of times. I had a tourist map and it showed you could go up into the valley behind the town and down to the waterfront again on the other side. But tourist maps don't give you much idea of ups and downs. It was a steep climb. I found myself up by the cemetery behind the *ancienne ville*—the medieval town—and next minute I was looking down over the Baie de Garavan. It was midwinter, late afternoon of a clear sunny day, and there it all was, laid out—a large part of what was to be my scene. Below and to the right there were the yellow walls and orange tiles of the old town. Further down, right away down in fact, almost as if it was below my feet, the waterfront road and the new swimming beaches and breakwater—beautiful pieces of public works, empty and waiting for the summer. Along the waterfront road, following east towards Italy—that was the village of Garavan. The railway followed the same direction as the road, but a contour higher. Then further up ran the Boulevard de Garavan—the road I was standing on; and higher still the terraced hillslopes rose more and more sharply at the same time pressing in towards the waterfront so that just beyond Garavan and the frontier post dividing France and Italy the rock faces, orange and pink and grey in the changing light, hung directly over the sea. Beyond again it all stretched away, dwindling in the fading afternoon—San Remo, Italy; another place, a different story.

The apartment at Garavan was too big for me and I settled a day or so later for a small bungalow villa—all but a couple of rooms which the landlady kept for herself. It was back in town, up a hill and looking out over *centre-ville* to the sea.

The Garavan apartment I passed on to my compatriots Clifton and Toni Scarf who arrived in the town a few days after I did. Clifton had a year's leave from his university and he'd somehow got permission to spend it on the Riviera instead of in Paris or one of the big university centres. He'd brought Toni and the three kids with him, all the way from New Zealand. It was January. They'd spent a day in Paris cracking ice on puddles and then taken the night train south, and next morning they were having breakfast out of doors at a café near the station. I know that journey. You leave Paris up to its ears in fog, sleet, rain, everything winter can throw at you, and in the morning when the sun comes up you're already racing along the Mediterranean coast catching sight of green palms, white villas, red rocks, yellow mimosa, blue bays. Colours!—almost candy colours. But that impression can be misleading.

After their hot chocolate and croissants by the station Clifton phoned the Agence Bienvenue and Ernst Bergen came for them wearing one of his immaculate suits and driving his Lamborghini Muira. Bergen was the international Dutchman (but not genial like most of his compatriots), managing French, German, English with equal cunning, and passable Italian; buying, selling, letting real estate, and then, as if the profits weren't enough, sitting all summer, through Saturdays, Sundays, feast days and festivals, behind the bullet-proof glass of his *change*, swapping deutschmarks, francs, sterling, lire, any currency at all so long as the customer accepted his rates of exchange. He had an American wife and two kids somewhere up in the hills, and in his office one inscrutable local girl who might have been his mistress. There were only a few signs of strain but they were disturbing, like deep scars under make-up. He could never meet your eye, even in shadow and through his tinted glasses. Sometimes late in the afternoon when business wasn't brisk he sat outside on a canvas chair on the pavement and you could see he'd been drinking. He became insolent then, with a subtle suppressed rage that shook you up, so you might go away thinking Why does that Dutchman hate me so much? until it occurred to you that he hated everybody, himself most of all.

Bergen had made a mistake that day. Or his office girl had given him the wrong information. He thought I had taken the Garavan apartment and that the little bungalow villa was vacant. There was a ring at the gate and I went down and there he was with the carload of Scarfs he'd just picked up at the station. He was offering them the place I had taken.

I asked them all up and we sorted out the confusion. That was my first meeting with the Scarfs. We sat on my terrace drinking vermouth while the kids skated on the shiny floors. As they went I reminded Bergen about the Garavan apartment. It was a bit shabby, just about right if you were going to have three kids knocking into the walls, and it was big. Bergen drove them out there and I heard a day or so later they'd taken it.

Shortly after that the rain started. Not just a few passing showers. Real rain. It went on for days. The spiky plants shone, the feathery ones drooped with it. The sea lost its blue enamelled look. The English colonels and German businessmen and Parisian Jews wintering in the south disappeared from the waterfront. So did the band. I didn't mind. The South of France has its seasons, and the winter one is not the most appealing. Turning out on that promenade on a good day in January or February when the sun brings all the visitors out is like taking a stroll in an outsize geriatric ward. Just one street inland is a normal French town going about its winter business. One street inland is the Rue St Michel, and it was there, while I was trying to buy myself a car, that I met Toni Scarf in pouring rain hurrying along under a transparent umbrella, with a square of red silk over her black hair. The pavement is so narrow there you have to step into the street to let people pass; and the street is so narrow when you step into it you hold up the crawling cars.

Toni and I ran into one another. She said hullo and we both stepped into the roadway.

Deck Chairs on the Riviera
1978

'We're holding up the traffic,' she said, and we stepped back on to the pavement.

'Now we're holding up the pedestrians.'

I steered her into a doorway. 'Do you speak French?' I asked.

'Oh yes,' she said. 'Well, a little. . . .'

'You don't know what a luggage rack's called, do you?'

'A . . . a which?'

'On a car. A luggage rack.'

'Oh yes. A roof rack. I think I do. It's a . . . .' She thought for a moment. 'It's "une galérie de bagages".'

I had been looking for a house called 'La Cour'. I'd been up and down the Rue St Michel three or four times asking shopkeepers but either they didn't understand me or they hadn't heard of it. It was the home of an architect called Hirondelle who owned a Fiat Dino I'd decided I wanted to buy. I'd seen it parked in a big garage off the Avenue Edouard VII and a young man told me its owner left it there because he had a weak heart and couldn't drive any more. He wrote Hirondelle's address on a piece of paper and now I was standing in a doorway just across the street from a little paved square called La Place aux Herbes, listening to the rain and thinking of Toni Scarf, who had just left me there, with her black hair under red silk and great drops of rain skidding over the transparent plastic of her umbrella. And then, as if it swam up hazily through that film of wet plastic, I saw it right under my nose—in ornate lettering shallowly carved in pale yellow stone: 'La Cour'.

A stone passageway curved away from the street and opened on to a cobbled path with buildings rising on either side. The path led to a flight of stone steps. They took a sharp right turn and led up into a garden hung with huge leafless vines, brown-black in the rain. The last leaves still floated in a blue-tiled lily pool, drained but filling with rainwater. Two or three large trees grew up the face of the building which enclosed the garden on two sides. All the shutters were closed. In the angle formed by the two wings of the building there was an entrance and a stairway. I climbed the stairs, stopping at each landing to look at the names on the doors opening off it, and then to look out at the garden with its brown vines and blue tiles and unswept paths.

At the top landing there was one door only and it was Hirondelle's. I rang and in a moment an elderly lady answered. I told her I had come about the Fiat. Her face was contorted for a moment by some strange convulsion but it passed. 'Entrez Monsieur,' she said. 'Laissez vôtre parapluie là-bas s'il vous plaît.'

I put my umbrella down where she pointed, wiped my feet and went in.

I didn't see Monsieur Hirondelle that first morning I called—he was unwell and still in bed. I had to call two or three times before the business of buying the car was settled. I remember the last visit (I had gone to hand over the money, which he wanted in cash) he told me a story— something that had happened to him during the war. I'm not sure why he told it. I'm not sure where it happened either. I see it as happening in one of the mountain villages behind the town—maybe Gorbio—but I don't think that can be right. Anyway Hirondelle was an officer and he'd retreated with his men into a village in the mountains. They sat out of doors in the little square eating and drinking and cracking jokes while away down towards the coast where the sea was glittering in the sun they could see little puffs of dust rising off the roads and that meant a German column coming after them.

They took their time and enjoyed the food and the wine and some time during the afternoon the first shells whistled in and the battle started. Hirondelle got separated from his men among olive trees on the terraces below the village. There seemed to be nobody about and then somewhere in front of him among the trees there was a German soldier and Hirondelle took aim and fired. The German reeled away, dropping his rifle, and began staggering down a track, and Hirondelle followed. The German kept staggering on and looking back, thinking that the Frenchman wanted to finish him off, but Hirondelle didn't have anything in his mind except maybe to take him prisoner. They came to a little valley with steep terraces on either side and whitewashed farm cottages deserted along a stream. The German was getting weaker. He crossed a bridge and slumped up against a wall in the sun. There was a little curved wayside shrine like an up-ended bath-tub with a painted madonna inside against a blue background. The German dragged himself to the shrine, dragged himself up to sit inside it in the shade. He didn't move again. He slumped back and sideways, held up by the shrine. Hirondelle waited. The sound of gunfire had died away. It was getting dark. There was only the sound of the stream running below the road. Hirondelle approached the shrine, watching for the least movement. There was no movement. The German soldier was dead.

It was the morning of the day I was to call on Hirondelle that I met Javine. I went into a café near the casino. It was almost empty, but a girl was standing with her hands on top of the juke box, nodding to the song that came from it. When it stopped she looked up and smiled. I invited her to come and sit with me.

She brought her cup of coffee to my table. She didn't speak a lot of English but we made our way in French. She told me she had lived all her life in the town (she pulled a face). Her parents had a small farm up in the hills but she had a little apartment in her uncle's house down by the fishing port. One day soon she was going to go and find herself a job in Paris. In the meantime she was doing a course at the university along the coast.

I asked her why she wasn't there today and she shrugged. The boredom, you know. Now and then one had to take a holiday.

She was a small neat girl with pale olive skin and very dark eyes so you expected black hair but it wasn't black, it was light brown, almost chestnut, but paler, like the colour of lager. She was slow, graceful, somehow withdrawn behind eyes that looked at you very directly, smiling. Everything was hidden but nothing was absent.

She played another record on the juke box. It was called 'Pour la Fin du Monde'—for the end of the world.

We parted in the street outside the casino. The billboard was advertising Walt Disney's *The Aristocats*, which had become *Les Aristochats*. I told her I was probably going to buy a car that afternoon and I asked her whether she would like to come for a drive.

When she looked up to answer she hesitated a moment, smiling, her mouth closed, her eyes full of intelligence, so that I felt, without knowing what it was I wanted to hide, that I was giving myself away.

I got to 'La Cour' at the appointed hour. The sky had cleared and the sun struck down among the heavy brown stems of the vines and lit up the grey stones of the old wall that enclosed the garden.

Madame Hirondelle showed me in and left me alone with her husband. This was our first meeting. He was sitting stiffly in his chair, carefully dressed and brushed. He excused himself from standing as he held out his hand. His breathing was heavy and his hand weak.

But he came straight to the point. 'You want to buy my car, Monsieur. The price is eight thousand francs. That is less than it is worth. My wife is not satisfied, but that is the price I have decided on. You see I can't get down the stairs to drive it. There is no lift. I am an architect, Monsieur, and I designed this building when I was young and fit. Pas d'ascenseur! Now if I went down those stairs I wouldn't get up again.' He smiled. 'The artist is trapped inside his design—isn't it so? And the price is right for you?'

I said it was right if the car was as good as it looked.

'You won't be disappointed,' he said. 'The young man from the garage has brought it over. He's waiting down in the car-park by the market. Perhaps you would like to go down to him?'

I got up to go. 'My wife believes you are some kind of artist,' he said. 'Is that so?'

I shook my head. 'I'm sorry to disappoint your wife.'

He smiled. 'She won't be disappointed. If she believes you are an artist you are an artist and that's that.'

'An artist manqué,' I suggested.

'I understand why you want my car,' he said. 'I used to be fond of it before my heart gave me trouble. The image of speed and power—it calls to us. I hope for you it will be a lucky purchase.'

'I'm sure it will,' I said.

Twenty minutes later I was driving up to Cap Martin, the *garagiste* beside me. Up there on the heights I stopped and looked down at the town.

'Elle marche comme une rêve, n'est-ce pas?' the *garagiste* said.

'Like a dream,' I agreed.

On the way back I called on Javine and asked her to come for a drive next day into Italy.

Just beyond Garavan are the frontier posts. You go through the French border guards, cross a white line marking the bed of a stream that runs under the road, and forward to the Italian guards. Clifton Scarf's kids used to get him to stop the car on the line so that Mummy and Dad in front were in Italy and the kids in France. Or they would get out and stand astride it, one foot in either country. It always seemed to me the moment I crossed that line I felt the change, like a sudden alteration in the weather. There was more poverty and more style; life was more primitive, more civilised, less bourgeois, more extreme. As the Fiat gathered speed Javine's hair blew across my face. The cliffs dropped to rocky blue bays, the hillslopes rose in terraces or lifted abruptly to bald bluffs. Neither mountains of rock nor empty canyons had been allowed to present themselves as obstacles. Mile-long tunnels succeeded one another, and between the tunnels, immense flyovers. Our path was direct, fast, mountains to the left, sea to the right, Genoa ahead, and beyond Genoa. . . . I couldn't find a word for what lay beyond, unless it was 'Tuscany'. It was a sense of space, freedom, movement, colour and light; or as if you travelled back into the womb and found its walls done out with frescoes by Botticelli.

Coming back to the town that evening I stopped at a rest area and Javine and I climbed down a path below the *autostrada* into a gully wooded with pines. It was quiet except for the calls of birds and the occasional whoosh of a car on the *autostrada* above. We held on to one another, steadying ourselves as we made our way down over uneven ground. Javine stopped and leaned back against the trunk of a tree.

Her head was back, her hair spreading against the rough bark, catching in it. She was wearing a leather jacket and the leather creaked faintly as she moved. I was aware of the curve of her breast just there under the flap of her jacket, and the shape of her jeans tight over thighs and crotch, and I had the thought that it was all there, available (if it was available) because I had just bought an old architect's Fiat Dino for which I would be paying eight thousand francs. It was as if some kind of absurd scruple had taken hold of me. Or was it just a lapse of confidence?

'You know,' I said, 'if it wasn't for my new car, you wouldn't be here.'

She screwed up her face, puzzled, as if she wasn't sure I was saying what I meant in her language.

'That is quite true,' she said. 'And neither would you, mon ami.'

OWEN LEEMING

Owen Leeming (b.1930), in his earlier years a widely published poet,
was last heard of in New Zealand letters in the mid-1970s. After
returning to Provence in 1972 from a year in Malaysia he bought
and restored a small village house and began writing in French. A
part-time job as a real estate agent was followed by two seasons as a
bridge and scrabble expert with Club Méditerranée, 'stimulated by
which' he wrote the unpublished novel Les Points Chauds *from*
which the following excerpt is taken. He now works in Paris as a
translator with the OECD.

The subject of Les Points Chauds (Trouble Spots) *is the love affair of*
a French agricultural expert in Africa with a Portuguese-born
woman in a context of student unrest. After the woman's
imprisonment in Africa the couple are finally reunited in Provence.

From Trouble Spots

Marseille-Marignane airport. 'Arrival of Air France flight number . . . gate number . . .' Black Africans in suits and ties, waxy-skinned whites waited behind the barrier to have their passports stamped. Where was Paula? Stéphane hoped he would recognise her when he saw her. The last through passport control was a woman wearing glasses pushing her two daughters ahead of her by the shoulders. No Paula. He felt stupid standing by himself in front of the passenger gate. Had he got the day wrong?

'You, what's your name?'

The policeman led him into a small office. Stéphane saw the eyes ringed with mauve, the lopsided lipsticked mouth, the skin of the head showing through the hair, the coat shoulders trembling.

'Do you know this person?'

'Yes.' It was a half-truth.

A policeman behind a desk raised his head and told the shivering overcoat, 'Report to the nearest Gendarmerie within eight days.' To Stéphane, 'Sign here.' Rubber stamp.

Stéphane collected two suitcases from Customs and loaded them on to the car.

'It's the same one,' murmured Paula. She pronounced it 'shame'.

The rain the curtains of spray thrown up by the wheels of lorries made it ridiculous for him to chat about the landscape. Robbed of small talk, Stéphane was forced to realise that what was sitting beside him had gone on a journey outside any atlas. He felt like a lumpen peasant, all body, no mind.

Paula had recognised only the eyes at first. His face had aged, but his general appearance was younger. His craggy solidity made her feel even more wasted. She would have liked to have recorded all her impressions, for memory, but her brain had lost the ability to concentrate.

The steady rain forced Stéphane and his 'guest' to stay inside the *mas*, now centrally heated. He did not feel brave or cruel enough to scrutinise Paula. The odd accidental glance had been enough to tell him what captivity had done to her: the dental prosthesis, the part-baldness, the darkened eye sockets.

Paula kept her coat on. She felt guilty. He had written 'Come' in ignorance of the kind of hysterical invalid he was inviting to stay. How many pretty women had he put off so that she could be there?

After dinner, he made her lie down on the settee. Seated next to her like a psychoanalyst, he told her to make her mind go blank and avoid talking. Tomorrow or the day after he would take her to see the doctor. When she had regained strength, he would show her the countryside.

Paula was happy not to talk. She looked up at the split old beams. She dozed and woke, sure she was in a dream. Silently, with her eyes open, she began to weep for all that had gone so wrong. Stéphane watched over his patient, feeling powerless as the tears ran from the corners of the bruised-looking eyes. She dropped off to sleep. He waited a while, then slipped his hands under the neck and knees of the sleeper and lifted up the damaged body. Placing his feet firmly on each step, he carried Paula upstairs and laid her on the double bed.

'This is for you. I'll be down below. Call me if you need me.'

He spread a blanket on the settee and tried to sleep. The idea that he had made love with that body seemed incredibly strange. He was pleased he could care for her. He turned his thoughts to his apple treelets.

The sun and the Mistral arrived together. Behind the wheel of the car, Stéphane wondered whether Paula's eyes could bear so much light. Wrapped in a blanket, she watched the passing rocks and twisted vegetation which he pointed out to her with an owner's pride.

'Look, over there, Sainte-Victoire, and that's the King's Pestle.'

Without their képis, the gendarmes looked quite human, but their message was not reassuring. They had received instructions concerning the status, or rather the lack of status, of Miss Paula Vouguès. She could stay in the country as a tourist for three months, then she would have to leave. Political asylum? That was a question for the Ministry of the Interior.

In the dentist's, the dermatologist's and the tropical disease specialist's waiting-rooms, Stéphane had time to think about other things than the staking and watering of his baby apple trees. He mused over the gap that had grown between his and Paula's lives. She was an incorporeal intelligence, while he had turned into an unthinking farm machine. Working on the land, he had stopped developing, whereas she would rise from the mouth of hell magnified and endowed with intimidating powers. He regarded himself as a clod-witted Frankenstein putting together a superwoman.

When Paula saw Stéphane coming back to the car from the chemist's shop, she smiled properly for the first time, showing her new incisor, canine and two molars. He was loaded with as many bags as though he had been to the supermarket.

On a bright sharp day without wind, Stéphane took his protégée on a tour of the places and monuments he himself was keen to see. He was once again the owner of the region. Paula

Femme Fatale, Paris
1978

learned about the architecture of the Provençal farmhouse, and listened to a *Guide Michelin* description of a Gallic city dedicated to the goddess of hygiene. She was tipsy with cypress-trees, sandy-coloured stone, and tiles mottled with lichen. The sight of a flock of sheep in an arid field with their old shepherd and his two dogs made her nearly ill with pleasure. She bravely trudged behind Stéphane to look at a ruined abbey. The smell of lavender and thyme rose from under their shoes. Not far from the abbey, they came across a romanesque chapel built in the form of a clover leaf and surrounded by slots cut into the rock of the ground. Stéphane threw himself into one of the tombs, closed his eyes and crossed his hands on his chest. He rose hurriedly from the dead.

'It's cold in there! But look at you, you've got roses in your cheeks.'

That evening, after the meal, he tried to give Paula a chronicle of what the world had been through since he had last seen her. She was surprised by his emphasis on the American setbacks in Vietnam. She had certainly missed an exceptional year. In the short spell between her release and her exile in the desert, she had read a few journals and her sister had told her something about the events of May in France. But she knew practically nothing of Czechoslovakia, the murder of Robert Kennedy, the voyage of Apollo 8 around the moon, the war of secession in Nigeria, the guerilla campaign in Portuguese Guinea.

The tomato-grower, reservoir builder, planter of twenty-three thousand apple tree saplings did not feel he was the ideal witness of his time. Paula was exhausted by his narration, not because it was boring, but because her head was racing like a mad scientist's laboratory, cascading sparks, flashing lights and dials. What a subject, the transformation of de Gaulle's régime, even more interesting than the great man himself.

'I shall take my pills and try to go to sleep, although I feel too excited for that. Thank you for a magnificent day. Good night, big man.'

The second month of Paula's stay came and went without any news from the Prefecture of the Ministry of the Interior. Later than usual, owing to the frost and snow, the almond blossom buds swelled and the gorse flowers opened timidly.

One day while shopping in town, Stéphane came across Chantal. Luckily he was unaccompanied. Her tone was sweet-and-sour.

'So Monsieur has no time left for his friends?'

That hurt, because he still felt a complex desire for Chantal . . .

ALLEN CURNOW

*Allen Curnow (b.1911) is New Zealand's most distinguished poet
and editor of two influential anthologies. Until 1976 he taught at the
University of Auckland and holds the LittD degree from that
university, and an honorary LittD from the University of Canterbury.
He has read and recorded his poems for major American universities
and the Library of Congress, for the BBC and Australian radio, and
for the Poetry Society (London) and the Cambridge Poetry Festival.
Author of more than twenty volumes, he won the 1988
Commonwealth Poetry Prize, received the Queen's Gold Medal for
Poetry in 1990, and a Cholmondeley Award from the Society of
Authors in 1992.*

Do Not Touch the Exhibits

A gulp of sea air, the train
bites off a beach, re-enters the rock.
A window, a blind cathode, greyly reflects,
Plato sits opposite, his nose in a map.
Where you're going's never what you see

and what you saw, is that where you went?
Is there a reef with an angler on it
whose rod makes a twitching U?
Has he landed his fat silver-gilt
dorado, smack! on a pan in the mind?

Why can't I cut corners and have them?
Daylight chips in again, with cypresses,
olives, loquat (*nespola* the Japan
medlar, not the one you eat rotten,
the other sort, butter-yellow, sweet

embedding slippery outsize pips),
artichokes, the native littoral

cultivations, rivermouth litter,
punctured cans, plastic bottles,
and behind (supposedly) the weatherish

pink and chrome villas gingerly
seated, shutters to seaward,
the Ligurian blue, too much of it.
Or weathering the long cape
another fisherman whose limping

boat I'm overhauling? a file
of red and white Martini sunbrollies
wheels in, peels off, drops back.
A brace of NATO frigates present
unmuzzled guns, 'optional extras'.

Beachcombings, introjections,
best stuffing for tunnels. Venus
on her lee-shore *poco mosso*
paroled from the Uffizi, screwed
to the wall under the baggage rack,

space reserved in the mind, goes
where I go, my side of the glass
beneath which our family motto's pinned,
è pericoloso sporghersi
indelibly incised on steel.

Rapallo, London
1983

Gare SNCF Garavan

The day doesn't come to the boil, it guards
a banked-up flame under a cool first light.
Madame tethers her Siamese to the doorway
of the Gare SNCF, the shadier side
of the tracks where we mustn't stray.

The tracks are bare, the pines don't stir, the haze

is international, Cap Martin is a thing
in the mind's eye of 'that eternal sea',
Bordighera just one more. Behind the doorway
of the sanctuary, something rings, Madame is

answering. I am questioning a blossom of
some nameless yellow creeper over the excitements
of life on a warm wall. Pussy is overweight,
so is Madame, but active, panties and *collants*
hang from an upper room, over the yard side

of the Gare, the seaward, shaded by the dark
eyelashes of the pines in a light that is not
explicit. Landward the Alpes Maritimes lean
scarily steep-to, by the Gare clock
I can relax, nobody's yet begun saying

'to the mountains, fall on us', only indistinct
voices drop from the lemon-gardens, the villas.
A frequent service. Madame emerges, bearing her
official baton, producing a train from Nice,
Italy's minutes away, an old-fashioned thought,

an old-fashioned iron expostulation of
wheels, fluttering doors, interrupts nothing.
So much at risk, a miracle that so much gets
taken care of, Madame picks up her cat from
the *quai* and cuddles it, conversing with friends.

Menton, London
1983

Sunset, Cassis
1991

SPIRO ZAVOS

Spiro Zavos was born in 1937 in Wellington, of Greek parents who migrated to New Zealand in the 1930s. Before he went as a boarder to the convent school at Seatoun, Star of the Sea, he spoke only Greek. Faith of Our Fathers *began life as a short story, 'The Shilling', and was expanded in Menton, a time during which New Zealand memories seemed 'particularly vivid'. The novella won a NSW Premier's Award in 1983.*
For the last decade Spiro Zavos has been a leader writer, book reviewer and rugby columnist for the Sydney Morning Herald.*

From Faith of our Fathers

There was no one in the restaurant when Stathos pushed open the dining room door and went inside. The tables were all set for the evening trade. The white napkins stood up like pyramids. Each table had a small vase with some daisies in it. The knives and forks and the tomato sauce and the vinegar and the salt and pepper shakers were all in place. Stathos walked down the carpet running down the middle of the dining room (the tables were on either side of the carpet for the room was a long and narrow one). He skirted the big wooden dresser which carried all the account books of the restaurant and stood at the end of the dining room proper. There was no cup of tea on the table near the dresser which his father sat at to go over the accounts with the accountant or to relax when business was slow and he had nothing to do for a while.

The little room in front of the kitchen where the coffee and tea stands were and the till where the bill for the meals was totalled and put on to the plate was also empty. The room smelt pleasantly of ground coffee. Stathos pushed into the kitchen. His foot slid on the slippery cement floor. There was nothing on the long iron oven, although through the grate he could see the orange-red glow of the burning coals. On the table running the length of the kitchen he could see the result of hours of work by his father. A huge tin bowl was filled with finely chopped lettuce. Another bowl, about half the size, stood beside it and contained mayonnaise that had just been made. The sweet-sour smell of it still lingered in the air. Several piles of dishes, plates of various sizes, stood near the end of the table. The sink on the far wall was empty and a number of grey cloths hung from the taps.

Stathos walked quickly through the kitchen, past the machine with hoses leading into the top and which peeled the potatoes, into the toilet and storage area. The winch was at rest on its hook and the upper loft was almost covered with sacks of vegetables. Beneath the loft there was a large sack of oysters. Lying on the sack was a red rubber mitten and a small knife with a dirty brown curving blade. A bucket beside the sack was half filled with the grey white blobs of oysters and another bucket, larger in size, held the empty shells. Stathos cautiously pushed open the toilet door.

It was quite dark inside the little chamber that led on to the toilet. Stathos made out the shape of his father squatting on what appeared to be a bowl. As his eyes became accustomed to the gloom he saw that steam was rising from the bowl. His father had his shirt open and Stathos could see his white chest and small forest of white hairs on it.

'What are you doing?'

There was no reply from his father. He sat quietly on the bowl, clutching its rim to steady himself. He had a morose look on his face. 'Eggplant poisons for haemorrhoids,' he said after some time. 'My arse is giving me hell. I felt buggered. It's a proper Greek remedy. None of your Kiwi medicines.'

When the water turned cold and the vapours stopped rising, he stood up and pulled up his trousers slipping his braces across his shoulders. He went across to the bench, struck a match and lit a piece of cotton wool that was lying inside a small bottle. 'Seeing you're here, you may as well be useful,' the old man said. 'Stick the top of the bottle on my back. Make sure you shift it around after a few seconds or you'll pull off a hunk of flesh.' Stathos did what he was told. The old man grimaced and sighed from time to time. 'Ah that's good. Just right.' He turned to Stathos, 'The chest now for a little while.' The cotton wool burned away. Stathos put the glass down. 'Grab my skin at the back and try to sort of wring it out. Like pushing clothes through the wringer. You understand.'

Stathos grabbed the white, baggy skin on the back of the old man, (he was surprised at his small sloping shoulders, he thought of his father as a bigger man than this) and he twisted and screwed the skin until it turned a red colour. 'That'll do boy,' his father said after a time. 'Let's go and have a cup of tea while there's a bit of time to sit down.'

The tea was strong, a dark brown thick colour, even with milk in it, and very sweet. His father was in a rare talkative mood so Stathos let him make the conversation. He started to talk about the strike and how it had affected business. 'Business no good, right now. Nobody's got any money.' Then he went on to say that he didn't understand what it was all about. 'The trouble is that Mr Holland and Mr Walsh, he's had meals here, a good man, aren't stupid. Your uncle Gerrie tell me that Mr Hill isn't stupid. Who is a poor fish and chip shop owner to believe. You tell me that one. You're the educated one. What's the answer, eh.' Before Stathos could venture an answer, his father pushed on. 'Want to know the trouble with this country.' He paused for effect and sipped loudly from his cup. 'The trouble is if you ask me, too many foreigners. When I came to this country twenty or so years ago, it was a great place. There were only a few Greeks and the rest, Kiwis. Never saw a Maori. Now you see them everywhere, except when they waitress for you and never turn up. Very bad. Very bad. And all the foreigners. Don't mind the Chinese, they're clean and keep to themselves. But the Indians are dirty. And the English, always drunk in the restaurant. Always after a free feed.'

'What about New Zealanders?'

His father drained the last of the tea. 'You never take any notice of me boy, perhaps that's all right. You're an educated boy. I left school when I was eight. Anyway, take my advice. Be careful of Kiwis. They'll try to take you down with the rest of them. They'll be nice to your face and behind your back they'll be throwing off at the fact that you're Greek. Mark my words.'

When everything was finally finished that night in the restaurant, around eleven-thirty, the

Seated Woman, Paris
1990

small family of father, mother and son, walked home through the deserted city streets. The old man was still talkative. 'See what I mean about business,' he said. They were walking past Carter's Wool Store towards the Dixon Street flats. 'How many people tonight, thirty, remember during the war the place was packed. We worked like slaves but made plenty of money. Missus was quicker than anyone in changing dollars from the American boys. They were terrific chaps those American boys.' They were climbing the Dixon Street steps. The old man paused after the second flight of steps to get his breath back. He turned his back on the flights rising above him. The city spread out before him, a dark ooze of black in the near foreground, the street lights marking a thin yellow trail through this and to the left a patch of sea shimmering under the light of a full moon and in front the sharply rising thrust of Mount Victoria that crouched over the city a vast, brooding watch dog. The old man surveyed this scene breathing heavily. When his breath came back, regular and lighter, he turned wearily and began to climb the next flight of steps. 'Your mother was hard to beat in those days,' he went on. 'A real help.' He looked across to the round-shouldered, silent woman walking beside him. 'Great days weren't they, Missus.'

The woman did not reply.

JAMES MCNEISH

James McNeish (b.1931) is a widely published novelist, biographer and playwright whose works include Mackenzie, Lovelock *and* The Man from Nowhere & Other Prose. *He has travelled extensively in Europe and in Israel and lived in London, Sicily and Berlin; from 1974-82 he was founder-director of the educational trust Bridge in New Zealand. The first of three volumes of his 'fictional autobiography',* My Name is Paradiso, *is soon to appear.*

Not So Far From Godwit Bay

Fouan Roussa
above Eze-village
French Riviera
May 1973

In Godwit Bay one of our neighbours had the early morning habit of strolling onto his verandah with a shotgun, aiming it at the swamp and opening fire. Sometimes he got a pukeko for breakfast, sometimes he didn't. He used to wake us with the noise. Here on the Avenue of Red Devils, which is the official address of this hilltop, we are also woken by explosions. They come from the woods on our right.

'Birds,' says M. Jacqueline, the landlord. 'They are shooting down birds.'

But it can't be birds. The local variety—têtes noires, cap-en-air, maisonges—are too small to feed a mouse, the pigeon-shooting season hasn't yet begun and in any case Princess Rainier is supposed to have stopped the annual massacre of wild pigeons flying in from Italy.

Later, going into La Turbie, I discover that the bangs come from a nearby quarry. There are quarries everywhere. The French have a nice habit of quarrying. First they sell the stone to the builders at Monte Carlo. Then, such is the demand for building sites, they sell the hole. The French are very clever.

The English here (unlike the French, who ignore you) sort you out rapidly. From La Turbie to Menton where we are expected for a lunch party is a 15-minute drive. We arrive late. Our hostess introduces us to the wife of a retired colonel who exclaims, 'Ah! You've got a Fellowship, I hear.' She adds, 'From Australia too. What is the aim—to deprovincialise?'

Peter and I are puzzled. Lunch consists of quiche, quenelles and there is good wine. But all the talk is of money and poverty. Our hostess for example says that everyone is badly off. I notice she has a French dishwashing machine that takes three soaps, including a special soap

46

for wine glasses that turns them out, as she says, 'glowing'. There are three or four families here. One family has just returned from skiing in Switzerland; another is just going skiing in Switzerland. I overhear a former actress, a redhead, ageing but still compelling, tell Peter that when he died her Papa left her 'eighty-eight glasses'.

'Eighty-eight? That's a lot.'

'No, no, dear. Not eighty-eight glasses all together. Eighty-eight of each type.'

It must be getting hard, Peter says maliciously, with the pound the way it is, to live here.

'Indeed,' the husband says. 'Some of the older English people here are living on just their annuities. Well. I shouldn't be surprised if they're not experiencing real hardship. I mean, *real* hardship.'

Over lunch the conversation turns from money to the weather. 'What is it like,' someone says, 'out on that hilltop where you are?'

'Lovely,' Peter says. 'Lovely and misty. It is like living in a cloud.' It is quite true. We have had swirling mist every morning; then the mist clears and the Mediterranean shines through.

'It's so nice to have bad weather,' I say. 'The other day we had snow.' Also (but I didn't say this) one morning it actually blew. The wind blew for half an hour and stopped.

Peter said: 'Yesterday it rained. At five o'clock. And M. Jacqueline, our landlord, who has been watering the garden every day, walked in the rain bare-headed and whistling.'

Queer looks all round the table. I think they think we are making it up. In Menton, where the English colony dwells, the sun shines on 300 out of 365 days and there has been, reportedly, one foggy day in the last ten years (eleven years in Cannes).

At some point we apologised to our hosts for being late.

'The traffic, of course,' they said.

'No, not the traffic. It is our clocktower. We have a clocktower.' In New Zealand where we usually lived, I explained, we overlooked a swamp and Ernie's singlets hanging out to dry, but on the hilltop above Eze where we lived now we overlooked a Saracen clocktower.

'In the morning we can read the time,' I said, 'without getting out of bed. It plays a tune.'

'You mean a carillon.'

'That's right. Now according to our landlord, M. Jacqueline, during the war the clock in the tower was always seven minutes fast—because of the hot air blowing from Italy. *Le souffle de Mussolini*. After the war, on July 1st, they fixed it. It is now seven minutes slow and we are seven minutes late for everything. That's why,' I said, 'we were late for lunch.'

'You poor dear,' the colonel's wife said, as we parted. 'You really must come into Menton more often.'

May 15

One reason we dislike driving into Menton is that whenever we do, and are separated, Peter gets picked up by old roués and invited to lunch. Of course they are all on holiday and are bored. Today an elderly gentleman with a toupée (Frenchman? Englishman?) followed Peter down an alley. She advanced. He performed a blocking movement. They danced a pas de deux and Peter fled to a beach where she sat on a wall, eating an ice. Then he came and breathed on her.

Another reason is that between us and Menton are 12 km of twisting motorway, or murderway as the locals have it. Each night on French television they take a town off the map. Last night it was a town called Mazamet, population 16,000: 16,000 was the road death toll in France last year. First they showed the map of France with the town taken out. Then they showed the town with its 16,000 inhabitants lying dead in the streets. Very effective. Peter was impressed. She said she is going to do an H.G. Wells and never, never drive in France.

Mind you, the reason H.G. Wells didn't drive in France was because he dared not: he said the temptation to run over a priest would be too strong.

Menton is stifling. From Menton we return to our hilltop, to the fig and cherry trees in thick leaf, as to an eyrie. There are nightingales at night, even cicadas—I mean real cicadas. (A nearby hotel has an electric one which chirrups in the rose bed for the benefit of tourists.) There is nothing ugly here. Not even the rockfaces, which are wired against landslides, are ugly. Peter calls them rocks with hair nets on.

The air is so fresh, the view so limitless that it seems unfair that M. Jacqueline's goldfish, which is called Wilberforce and inhabits a sunken pond outside our kitchen, cannot see it. Does one *never* get a headache on the Riviera?

20 May

One of the people we met at last month's house party was a Colonel White, known as Tiger White. Last year Tiger White organised a rugby match between Menton and the English town of Rugby. He said the rugbyites of Rugby chartered two planes. They came in blazers and club ties and Menton didn't sober up for three days.

'You do know,' he said, taking my arm, 'that the founder of rugby is buried here?'

I had forgotten about William Webb Ellis.

Today, on my way to Garavan, I visited the Menton cemetery. I couldn't find the tombstone at first because my Italian guide got lost. Eventually I found it. It is just below the Russian Chapel.

The tomb is inscribed:

> Rev. William Webb Ellis
> late Rector of St. Clement Danes Church, Lon.
> (died 24.2.1872)

and:

> This stone commemorates the exploits of
> William Webb Ellis who
> with a fine disregard for the rules of football
> as played in his time
> first took the ball in his arms and ran with it
> thus originating the distinctive feature
> of the rugby game
> AD 1823

The stone was presented to Menton by Rugby School last year. On it, wilting, lay a wreath, deposited by a group of travelling referees.

A French source tells me that the early games of rugby had no referee, no rules and 20 players. They took the form of pitched battles. Tiger White's game, I gather, was a little like this. According to my French encyclopaedia on sport, le rugby (before it crossed the Channel) was 'a huge mêlée from which the ball rarely appeared'. Peter says, looking over my shoulder, it would be a good idea if the Mansfield Trust, which has sent us here, got together with Rugby

The Waitress at Arles
1980

School and promoted a Scholarship for Rugby-Playing Writers. As a former rugby coach myself, I agreed.

Actually although the brave rector 'took the ball in his arms' as early as 1823, rugby didn't cross the Channel to France until 1887 (or eight years after tennis crossed). While on the subject: I did ask Tiger White, 'Who won last year's game between Rugby and Menton?' I asked him twice. He wouldn't tell me. Since then I have been reliably informed that the French haven't lost a game against the English in 15 years.

As to how the game is actually *played*, my French encyclopaedia doesn't say. It describes the game as 'apparently complicated'. It adds, 'Of all sports, rugby most resembles the simple games of children, cops and robbers, cowboys and Indians and many others of the kind.' Vive la France!

end May

Today I offered to cut the grass for M. Jacqueline. He seemed momentarily stunned, as if by contemplating physical labour on the Riviera I had broken a law. All the Jacquelines' tenants— our neighbours are Parisiens, a Polish aristocrat and a Belgian couple who spend the day washing their car and admiring the view—are here on holiday.

I insisted. M. Jacqueline sighed. Eventually he produced a sickle. It was rusted. He sharpened it by rubbing it on the crook of his arm and said, 'Voilà'. I used it. After I had been cutting the grass with it for two hours, the hillside was unchanged.

I returned the sickle. M. Jacqueline was under a tree, bent double, using a scythe. He stood up whistling, through bunkered teeth, a wiry man in soft-soled shoes and wispy hair. He began to talk of the Death of the French Countryside.

'Do you know,' he said, 'my wife and I drove 120 kilometres the other day—voyez-vous, 120 kilometres. All we saw were three ancients, two old men and a woman. And a few goats. Empty! The countryside is empty! Now when I was in England and Wales and in Sussex, it was very different. The English—ah, the English have survived the Industrial Revolution. The French have been crushed by it.'

He leaned on the scythe. I didn't tell him that in England only 2% of the population was left on the land.

'Civilisation,' he said. 'Civilisation is the curse of France! It has made the French dry up inside. They no longer use their brains. They no longer have any brains to use. It is tragic.'

He filled the wheelbarrow and pushed it a few yards. 'Do you know,' he said, coming back, 'that civilisation is a worse threat to France than communism.'

I hadn't realised until then, but his attitude is not so very different from that of the English on the Riviera, or any of the moneyed foreigners who have villas here. Of course they, hearing the thick patois, noting the rough hands, make the mistake of putting a label on him—peasant. But M. Jacqueline is not a peasant. He is a Normandy farmer, as fiercely independent as they. The difference is that he is rooted in the soil and his patriotism, his loss of pride in France, is a terrible thing.

'Do you know,' M. Jacqueline says. He always walks away with his wheelbarrow and then comes back. 'Do you know that the local farmers round here, illiterate men, men who have had schooling only until 10 or 11, they could read. I have seen them and they could read. They did read. Today? The people in the towns, do they read? Bah. It is tragic.'

I told him that in the south of Italy it was the same. I had met Italian peasants who had taught themselves to read and to think. The same. But this is small comfort—M. Jacqueline is off again about the decadence of France.

I stopped him. 'M. Jacqueline,' I said, 'you are wrong. France has writers, it has inventors and philosophers. It has thinkers.'

'Ah but,' he said. He sighed, and this time he sighed deeply. 'They are all *on the Left*.'

Summer 1973

News from New Zealand: Our cat Dolittle, whom we left with a farmer in the Waikato, is apparently putting on weight. Dolittle has eaten three sheep, he says. Minced. There is also a letter from our district nurse in Tarahill. Nurse is strong on homemade bread, and we had written telling her of the French varieties, the various shapes and sizes, including one loaf that is called Gina Lollobrigida. Nurse writes: 'Ask them have they got a Sydney Flat?'

I thought of nurse today when we called on Miss Campbell. Miss Campbell lives in Menton and has 12 cats. Nurse also has 12 cats, but there the comparison ends. Miss Campbell, whose first name is Rosebud, is in her 70s. She lives with her gardener and her cats on the Boulevard de Garavan above the old town of Menton and the cathedral, and Rosebud Campbell has been in Menton for so long she can remember Katherine Mansfield. This is why we have called.

'Mansfield?' she says. 'In Menton? Oh well, Menton has had its day of novelists. We had one writer who came here called Mabel Barnes Grundy and she wrote "Patricia Plays a Part" ... Katherine Mansfield, yes. I remember seeing her when I was a girl—from the back. I only saw her from the back. She wore a sort of monk's habit and was alone. I always called her the Invisible Woman.'

Rosebud Campbell isn't really interested in Mansfield. She is interested in introducing us to her cats. One is called General de Gaulle, Charlie for short. Another is the hundredth offspring of a cat called His Eminence. Each day, Miss Campbell says, a maid comes at four to feed the cats and put them to bed. As I say, there are 12 cats.

But that is nothing, she says, to the situation at Eze-village. 'In Eze-village there are cats and cats and *cats*. There are so many cats that the local population can't feed them all, they have to be fed by an overseas foundation. There is an overseas gentleman who comes regularly, I understand, to arrange it.'

Peter and I exchange glances. Eze-village is just at the foot of our hill and we have never noticed any cats there. Mind you, we have never been there, except once to a restaurant and the meal, as I remember, cost the equivalent of a month's remittance for my fellowship. Eze-village, like so many picturesque villages along the Côte, is a tourist trap. It is not a village, it is a museum. The stone houses are charming, with their flower pots and vigne vierge climbing over wrought-iron balustrades, but the cobbled streets are empty, void of human and animal life.

Cats?

'She would hardly tell a lie,' Peter says. 'Would she?'

Later, we stroll down our hillside and wander, surprised, through the Saracen streets of Eze-village—for Rosebud Campbell is right. Eze-village is overrun by cats. They are behind every flower urn, on every balcony, round every fountain, in every doorway. They are French cats, mind. French cats are not like Italian cats, and less like Jerusalem cats. Italian cats pounce and scream, Jerusalem cats nudge and leer. French cats are squashed in at the back and look the other way. They are silent, also snooty. I have never succeeded in stroking a French cat. They have a knowing air, like French women. As we approach, the cats of Eze-village back off. Perhaps they have always done it, like the peasant women whose ears are pierced from childhood and hung with small tight gold earrings. This hasn't changed. Perhaps it is not the French cheese after all, but the French cat which is the symbol of an unchanging countryside.

One other thing about the alley cat of Eze-village. It is not hungry. It may be silent and never purr, but it is never in doubt. It knows where the next meal is coming from. I checked on Miss Campbell's story, and she is right again. There is indeed a foundation. The cats of Eze-village are fed by an overseas trust. The trust is American. The gentleman who comes once a month to pay the cats' money into an account is Swedish. He is called the *Directeur des Chats*.

25 June
Mark, who is studying to pass U.E., claims we are the only three-typewriter-family on the Côte. Peter is writing a book with her machine, I am ditto with mine and Mark is using a brokendown model with a continental keyboard in an effort to matriculate with the Correspondence School in Wellington. So far he is prospering, even showing enthusiasm, a tribute to his anonymous teachers who appear in three months to have galvanised him more than three years of state schooling ever did.

But he is puzzled about the German course. His German teacher seems to think he is on a trade mission to Berlin. His last assignment contained this warning:
ADVICE TO YOUNG BUSINESSMEN
You would be ill advised to speak of the Second World War. Everyone will be pleased if you complain about the Berlin Wall.

1 July
Today Mark got a genuine shock. In La Turbie, where we had gone to mail his fortnightly assignment, I noticed a sticker above the mail slot. It said:
'Attention! The Postal Service with the Antipodes is Suspended.'
Mark blanched. We went to the counter. We stood in a queue for half an hour and then Mark said to the woman behind the desk: 'What about my Correspondence papers?'
'The service is suspended, monsieur. It is a political matter, monsieur.'
I said, 'When will the service resume?'
The woman at the desk shrugged. 'Who knows, monsieur? Perhaps never.'
Apparently the suspension is in retaliation for an Australian trade union ban in protest at French nuclear tests in the Pacific.
Peter said: 'It's as if they've taken Australasia off the map. It's just like wartime.'
I said, 'No. It's just like Godwit Bay.'
In Godwit Bay, whenever the launchman went on strike and refused to take our mail, we would resort to subterfuge in order to get it to the mainland. Over the years it went out in a variety of containers, disguised as laundry, dry cleaning, geological samples, freight of various kinds. Once it went out in a violin case and once the dog doser took it in a hydatids bag. My last book manuscript travelled the first leg of its journey from Godwit Bay to London in a trans-Tasman yacht.
Here it is more difficult. Subterfuge won't work.
We sat on the seafront and racked our brains. Mark said: 'There don't seem to be any yachts going to New Zealand.'

9 July

French post offices are infuriating at the best of times. They smell. They are old and the queues endless. The employees are so overworked they have to stand, their backs to the customers, and tear at pieces of pizza with their teeth in order to get a lunch break. At least they do in Nice. Today we were summoned to the post office at Eze-sur-Mer to collect a book, mailed from Paris, which weighed an ounce or so over 1 kilo. It took an hour to clear the parcel. If it had weighed just under 1 kilo, the girl said, 'it might have been delivered to you'.

Might?

'Yes. What happens is that the parcel mail from Paris comes by rail and then by lorry as far as Eze-sur-Mer. And sometimes, if the lorry is overheated, monsieur, it cannot get up the hill to Eze-village. It is a very steep hill, monsieur. Only yesterday,' she said, 'one of the tourist coaches was left on a curve. All the passengers had to get down and walk.'

I said, 'I think the French post office is the most infuriating institution in the world.'

'C'est ironique,' she said, and gave a little smile. 'How ironical you should say that. Everyone finds it difficult.'

But back to the Pacific.

On ORTF, the French broadcasting service, there is a blanket silence about the French nuclear testing programme. In the meantime, we have got round the mail problem by sending Mark's Correspondence work to London, NZ House. Thence it goes down under by diplomatic bag.

19 July

France exploded a hydrogen bomb in the Pacific yesterday. We learn this from the BBC. The BBC says the explosion was monitored by a NZ frigate in the zone which has our Defence Minister, Arthur Faulkner, on board.

No French news bulletin has so far mentioned the bomb.

Later, evening: ORTF radio news, in its first mention that anything unusual is afoot in the Pacific, alludes to 'foreign intervention'—meaning, I gather, Mr Faulkner and his naval frigate. ORTF calls the frigate 'that Pacifist ship'.

Next day

It must be the season of divine anger. French soldiers are on manoeuvres in the woods all round us—explosions all day. Not to mention pyrotechnical blasts at night from the direction of Monte Carlo. Has war been declared? Lightning the other night killed a fisherman in his dinghy, caused landslides near Mougins, blocked the Corniche in several places and fires broke out on the other side of Cannes.

Today at noon there was an eclipse of the sun. Our landlord, M. Jacqueline, ran out and watched from the hill, in some excitement, then he parked his wheelbarrow beside our terrace and sat down. He seemed disappointed. He said, 'It was only a partial eclipse. The centre was over Africa.'

He told me the last true eclipse was three years ago—all the birds fled, blinded, over the hill to the Corniche below. When it was over, they began to sing again.

They must have been genuinely struck dumb, I say.

He nods, cocking an ear. Above us, as we sit talking, the explosions continue 'Soldiers,' he mutters. 'Fools.'

I cannot make out if the military in the woods are playing at soldiers for the sake of playing at soldiers, or if they are playing at soldiers as a deterrent to would-be fire raisers and arsonists. Many of the fires here are deliberately started. The fires, with temperatures climbing to 36, 38, can be terrifying. There are very few woods left. They get fewer each season. Last week a pine plantation went up five kilometres from here. But why does M. Jacqueline call the soldiers fools?

'You don't understand,' he says. 'That fire last week was *caused* by the military. They were on manoeuvres. A grenade went off, bang. One tree caught fire, all the trees caught fire—and the soldiers had no equipment to put out the fire.'

He collects his wheelbarrows, his scythe, his stone and stands a moment on the terrace. In the distance, towards Cannes, smoke is rising. Another fire. I begin to see why M. Jacqueline spends every day trying to reduce the wild grass on this hillside to the level of stubble. A backbreaking job, with just an old scythe. I wonder why he doesn't get a mower.

'Fools!' he says again. 'The army, the military, all fools. They are not mechanised. If those soldiers last week had been mechanised, they could have put out the fire. Do you know that in the First World War, France had only carts? Horse-drawn carts! In the Second War it was the same. The French are behind in everything, everything.' He sharpens the scythe and goes off. Then he comes back.

'I hear that we exploded a nuclear bomb in the Pacific. Can it be so?' He says, 'I heard it on the BBC.'

Yes, well (I almost said). If the BBC said so, it must be so. I was thinking of those lines of Glover:

> *When the BBC announced the end of the world*
> *It was done without haste*
> *It was neutrally, gentlemanly done*
> *It was untinged with distaste.*
> *It was almost as if the BBC had won.*

'Yes, that's right,' I said. 'France set off a hydrogen bomb. But I don't think it was a very big bomb, or even a very new bomb. I heard it was a device invented by the Allies twenty years ago.'

'Ah,' he said, and nodded sagely. 'Voilà. It is just as I say. The French are always one war behind.'

BARRY MITCALFE

Barry Mitcalfe (1930-1986), lecturer, poet, novelist, publisher was among those in the 1960s and 70s who were instrumental in exposing a new non-Maori readership to Maori writing. A prolific writer and latterly publisher of his own and others' work through the Coromandel Press of which he was the founder, he laboured tirelessly not only to produce the books he felt to be important, but also virtually single-handed to distribute them throughout the country.

Uncle On—and Off—His Bike

For my next death, gravity and tax-defying act I will, said Uncle, ride the bicycle, so having caught his unsuspecting moped and grappled it to the ground Uncle, with great presence of mind, shouted, best of three and, taking it from behind, lurched one pace forward and two sideways, which is not only an inefficient, but a painful mode of progress, nevertheless, through a pretty blend of perserverance and pure idiocy, necessary to survival, if not travel on the bicycle, Uncle took to wheels like rotating credit or a building society salesman on commission or a man with both legs removed (Uncle was actually none of these) he was, if anything, happy (a purely temporary illusion) riding his bike along the wobbly line that separates excessive confidence from undue caution, taking his tired old eyes out to see the world, giving his utilitarian nostrils a whiff of its many parts, wrapping his elephantine ears around the various dings, dongs, creaks, squeaks, groans, moans, whistles and grizzles with which Nature greets the unwary cyclist as he makes his downhill runs (on uphill ones he can only hear the huff and puff of himself) until he comes at last like Columbus to the edge of the earth (on Ogle's Hill) where, carrolling through the hole in his beard, giving Nature a little of its own back, singing with all the subtlety and harmony of an antique heron-croak compelling attention for miles around and awe within a slightly more limited range, Uncle finds himself impelled by the moving hand of fate (or possibly gravity) inexorably onward and downward like New Zealand in the grip of Muldoon or progress itself, gaining for lack of any brakes something of the speed and trajectory of an earthbound rocket, breaking wind with all its parts, briefly flaring like the meteor to an instant death. Respectfully according himself the three minute silence in honour of the dead, Uncle goes one way, the road another. Ah, the pity of it, the utter superfluity, the instant weightlessness of a man in flight, stripped of all past encumbrance, totally solitary, screaming in a pure high C.

Uncle's Love Song

Once upon a tiddle-pom-pom, tiddle-pom-pom
Uncle rode into the sunset of Mrs Murgatroyd,
His guitar was loaded, playing rub-a-dub-dub
To her fiddle-de-dee, a merry old soul was he,
But not any more, said Uncle sadly, I'm just
A one-string base and that string slack. Yes,
said Mrs Murgatroyd, and Uncle's face fell—
One string, she said, but with a thousand tunes,
An Aeolian harp in a hurricane, a trombone sliding
From here to eternity, the 1812 Overture with
Atomic cannon. Possibly, said Uncle, picking up
His face. But not today. I feel like a clapped
Out two-stroke limping home for a last pit stop.
Never, said Mrs Murgatroyd, you're the original
World War One air ace on a dangerously low mission
Behind enemy lines, you hold the flying bedstead
Record, you are sun, moon and tides all in the one
Elderly scrotum. Uncle's smile became a frown—
Not elderly, said he, old, and at the end of my tether.
Ah, but what a tether, said she, if the world were
A billy-goat swung by its neck, that tether would
Go twice round the universe and swish all the stars
Aside. Oh, the pain of it, said Uncle, happily. It
Would cannon off the far cush and go down for a hole
In one. You've mixed your sports, said Uncle, primly.

Spring Flowers
1991

No, said she, there's only one sport and you are it.
You exaggerate, said he. Oh, I do, I certainly do, alas,
But wasn't it lovely while it lasted? Yes, said he,
And turning back to back, they slept, two faces
With one expression, wistful, contented.

Uncle Casts a Paper Dart

Beware of little men, Muldoonolini
Rowling-Bowling and Straight-bat Beetham
And that other fellow with the foreign name
Out to save the country from itself.

Campaigners large and small, diddlers, fiddlers
And little Tom-tiddlers all come knocking
On Uncle's door, for 1 day out of 1094
He has the vote, whatever that may mean.

It's a purely paper transaction, giving him
Promise of great wealth, these days they buy votes
With our own money, ten percent tax rebate, allow
Twelve percent inflation,—2%, that's what he gets

How it seethes, the body politic, those are not
Limbs that move, but worms; how sweetly sings
The busy blowfly, that early harbinger of spring
That fat little wizard of buzz, sings Uncle.

Exercise your vote. Others died for it, or so
The posters say. They was robbed, says Uncle stoutly
The same tired jockeys still whip their clichés
Past the post, but only one man can win.

A million proxy-riders and the usual motley band of
Place-getters claim the race. Punters go home
Sadder and wiser, but not for long. Optimism and
Corruption go on forever, sings Uncle.

He is an innocent, he is that survivor who
Slept through the holocaust and woke to find

Inexplicable laughter and tears. Rows of cabbages
Or bums on a bench in parliament, you get

What you deserve, sings Uncle, a plague on both
Your parties, I come to bury Caesar, not to vote
For him. Dogs may howl, but rotund, benign
The moon remains.

PHILIP TEMPLE

Philip Temple (b.1939), writer and photographer, is author of twenty books including Beak of the Moon, The Legend of the Kea *and* New Zealand Explorers: Great Journeys of Discovery. *He is the PEN representative on the Authors' Fund Advisory Committee and is on the PEN national council.*

Gens et Sites

19 September: Room still smells. Put all furniture outside for sun to burn off mould. Beat hell out of rug. Feel better. Problem with lavatory cistern but am luckier than earlier fellows— Anton Vogt tells me that Janet Frame had to use a bucket. Investigate Villa Isola Bella above and find loose shutter so can climb inside. Big cracks in the walls which lean dangerously. Terrace where KM used to dally is covered by weeds. Did she notice steam and smoke from locos thundering along railway just below? Fiona (12) and Roger (11) started school today at Condamine.

22 September: Menton is for the exclusive tourist and rich retired. *Nice-Matin* journalist thinks it highly amusing that NZ writer should come round the world to sit here in renovated garden shed and write, probably, about New Zealand. Enjoy food, wine and prospect of Italy, but concede cannot find connection between keas and Cocteau.

27 September: Following talk with journalist, decide that NZ presence in Menton needs a lift. It is, after all, *Anniversaire des 10 Ans d'Association entre la Nouvelle-Zélande et Menton par la Fondation de l'écrivain Kathérine Mansfield.* Sounds well put like that, especially in the enthusiastic tones of René Vial at the Syndicat d'Initiative who visualises something spectacular at the Palais de l'Europe at end of November. Suggest my travelling exhibition of South Island photos be brought down from London. Will see what NZ Embassy in Paris can add.

30 September: We take Kombi and go for weekend trip to Vallée des Merveilles. Marvel at rock drawings and nearby deserted villages. Decide to take short cut on way back via Ventimiglia in Italy. French border guards wave us through, then we drive down half a kilometre of gorge to find, because we have forgotten kids' passports, Italians will not let us enter. Desperate five minutes on way back through No-Man's Land. Will French also not let us back in? Wave

cheerfully at perplexed gendarme as we press on at speed past border post.

12 October: The bliss of writing beneath Villa Isola Bella: express trains, local trains, freight trains, some stopping quietly, some stopping with a nerve-rending shriek of brakes, some not stopping at all, such as empty steel freight wagons or tankers creating echoing reverberations of hellish noise, all within 40 metres of the window. A bulldozer 100 metres away is digging out a driveway for a new block of concrete flats from which carry the soothing tones of circular saw, hammer and compressor. There's the constant tooting of horns as cars and motorbikes negotiate the winds and narrows of the nearby road under the railway. Add the regular domestic noises of dogs, arguing Italians, people who chatter past the gate, people who try to get through the gate, the hum of traffic along the main Riviera highway, the occasional penetrating droné of turboprop airlines. Sometimes I can discern the songs of birds.

18 October: Embassy will send down books about NZ for exhibition and selection of documentary films. René organises main Palais theatre for free showings. Photo exhibition will be in salon by main entrance. The lamb war is hotting up. French farmers picking on NZ imports in EEC dispute. Suggest to Embassy that we put on proper reception for local dignitaries at exhibition opening—could be politically useful. Am told budget will extend to only a couple of bottles of gin.

23 October: Walk home from room to hear of domestic imbroglio (this seems the right word here). Daphne tells me that boy next door, who has been mooning over Fiona for weeks, tried to kiss her under lemon tree. Roger rushed in yelling, 'Mum, Mum! Alain's killing Fiona!' Not so—only the wrangling limbs, red faces and steaming frustration where pubescent desire meets pre-pubescent rejection. Surprising Roger didn't yell in French. He's doing well at the Condamine. Has the local accent to an *é*.

27 October: Vogts invite us round again for drinks. We had enjoyable day together last week in Monaco culminating in concert where Kiri sang Strauss's 'Four Last Songs'. She looked great but couldn't hear much because of bad acoustics. Today Anton is in his 'furious toad' mode. Insists we turn up early, before the McNeish's, because he thinks they want to purloin his Fairburn material. All a bit hysterical. Constrained and tense evening with everyone posing. Why am I here? Ask James McN. why they are looking for a home in Mediterranean, Cyprus in particular. Anton says because the wine and fags are cheap. McNeish says, 'Because I feel I no longer have anything to offer New Zealand.' I think I know what he means.

9 November: Writing not much good. But the sun keeps shining. Lamb crisis worse. Deputy mayor is a retired air force general, a rampant Gaullist. Take some care with what I say at Mairie about forthcoming NZ exhibition. Officials seem to view it with a trace of condescending amusement. Should not have mentioned the gin episode. Decide to present one of my photos, framed, to Mairie at conclusion of exhibition. A little prestige regained.

19 November: Visit casino at Monte Carlo. Roulette table surrounded by Ian Fleming characters—a fat, cigar-smoking Italian with wads of bank-notes in his hands and painted bimbo on his arm; a raddled, ruined, chain-smoking habitué, gambling away her *ennui*; a thin,

Café, Nice
1991

pale-faced addict with one last chip he cannot bring himself to throw on the table; a good-looking playboy nervously laughing away twenty thousand francs in twenty minutes. Don't have the courage to make a bet. All this at eleven on a Monday morning.

28 November: There are posters all over town—*Gens et Sites, Photographies de l'Ile du Sud de la Nouvelle-Zélande*. René has put my speech into French and M. Lemut, the mayor's assistant, goes on Palais stage to introduce me before first film showing. I hear him announce the Erebus plane crash—first I hear of it. Says Ed Hillary is dead. Concentration on speech buggered. Stumble through in shocking accent, mumbling about the special connection between NZ and the Pearl of France. Sense some sympathy out there under the lights. But not when films start showing. Lemut palpably stiffens beside me as the documentary 'The Grass Growers' reels on, showing shockingly green pastures, fabulous scenery and thousands of sheep. He leaves as soon as he is able, snubbing me. Feel much better.

13 December: *Nice-Matin* approves of the exhibition and films. As have most of the patrons, judging by their comments in the visitors' book. Good crowds. Hundreds of booklets on NZ disappeared within first few days.

17 December: We have rendezvous with deputy mayor to present framed photo of Milford Sound (chosen by librarian). Are made to wait. Greets us with barely controlled ire. He does not look at photo, briefly holds my hand. 'You must be pleased with your success, M'sieu Temple,' he chokes out. We are no longer needed. Leave feeling angry but elated. A victory indeed. The sheep win.

MICHAEL HARLOW

Michael Harlow (b.1938) is an American-born lecturer, poet, editor and composer whose collections include Nothing but Switzerland and Lemonade, Today is the Piano's Birthday *and* Giotto's Elephant.

Interior Decorating

The postcard, a photoprint, is in sepia tones and yellowing with age. Still, it is clear, you can see that—and looking beyond there is a splendid view of the Duomo and the Campanile; as you might expect, there is also a middle-distance view of the Baptistry.

When you look again—it is of course the figure standing in the foreground, in front of the South Door, who appears so remarkable: a young woman in a white dress with her arms raised in front of her. You imagine she has just then walked into the picture, and she is turning to say something, to her right, gesturing with her arms.

What is so extraordinary is that the very moment the picture has been taken, the shutter opening, there is a flock of birds, their wings beating the air for a nesting place in the uppermost part of her body, entirely obscuring her face.

At that moment—the photoprint and my friend's words coming together remind me what I had perhaps too conveniently set aside recently: that his girlfriend and once mine has been falling out of the world into herself for some time now.

From that city of light and dark, he writes that sometimes we fall into ourselves so completely that we can hear only the sound of ourselves thinking. A single sound.

Or is it the other way around?

She snaps her fingers in irritation, the girl, Marianina.

He is shaken by it, and he feels it. He is convinced, and it doesn't take long, that *she is trying to climb into heaven on her own, which is not good for her.* Is it?

But what can he do?

Can you imagine, he asks, not hearing a sane sound for years uttered by anyone but herself?

She is surrendering to certain signs so easily that what was once remarkable is becoming the stuff of commonplace—once you could glance up at the weathercock turning in the air, or the delicate print of trees against the sky and be touched by the wonder of it. Now—there are

Signs.

Pictures, really.

And the only words he hears himself saying return to him, their wings clipped.

The only measure, he insists, is to *hear* what you *see* before you've actually seen it. Then of course the seeing is a distinct possibility.

Don't you agree?

As you can see, my friend is a talker. He is also something of a philosopher by habit.

Worried?

Of course he is worried.

Would you not be worried, or even fearful when he makes it clear that his girlfriend is obsessed with *interior decorating*?

She keeps decorating the flat, right here in the middle of the city, in what she says are post-holocaust images.

I know that her mother was once a smalltown movie star, and her father in vaudeville, and there was an uncle in arts and crafts.

But—it cannot be altogether that.

Consider when they first settled in the city.

What was once to us a comfort is no longer: when you look out, when you look in, those domestic signs that were so consoling: women ironing frocks and gowns in lighted windows open to the river breezes; some small and sinewy gentlemen leaning into their mirrors, carefully waxing their moustaches for an evening on the town; and at almost any hour you can hear automobiles turning corners, people on their way to dinner or racing to a weekend in the country.

Now—there are certain darkening details; you see, it is altogether different.

She stays home all day every day late into the night talking about the *fatality in her mind*; pasting up those terrible pictures, one after the other, in all the rooms of the flat—even on the doorframes, the mirror borders, yesterday the ceilings, the day before the bare spaces on the floors, carpets and rugs rolled neatly into the corners.

Until, if you can imagine it, all the spaces in the flat have been bandaged against what she insists has been *a year of terrors, and where do you suppose God has got to in such a crazy hurry?*

There are so many of them that at first it is quite bewildering. You have to look carefully from room to room, and suddenly you realise that they are actual photographs torn from magazines, newspapers, and books . . .

There are pictures of bodies with open wounds, bright-edged gashes, bodies mangled and blasted apart without limbs without heads, bodies sometimes liquefied to a pulpy mass.

There is even the charred after-image of a running child pressed into the pavement. It could be a fossil-fact.

Soon, you begin to believe, don't you, that there may be no bodies at all—rather, a whirlwind of torn pages, and printed light.

And sometimes there is writing. On one page scrawled in greasy red crayon inside the hook marks of someone speaking: *Did you think the light could print all our desires? Even if light is the healer's true God?*

To which of course I have no reply.

But, it is true that I have given her flowers freshly cut, circus animals in rainbow-coloured tights from the stalls by the river, once even a singing bird happy in its cage.

And more.

I pleaded with her for a weekend in the country. On any windy day we could pitch a kite into the air, silk and paper, and let it fly. One way, wouldn't it be, to feel the wind shiver in the palms of your hands? And other wind instruments. One way to say something about love—an afternoon of intimate photographs in the countryside, the brushwork of trees and tall grasses, the smell of stones in the sun. But, no.

She refused straightaway, you see. She asks do I realise, after all, *that the gates to the future are being closed, if you think about it.*

What's more, she is convinced that on her daughter's wedding night *when a pillow falls it will break her ribs if not her heart.* And no occasion for dancing, is it? A delicate matter.

All the while she is bandaging the flat against some shadow in her heart.

After a while, I began to inspect the flat each day to see where she had got to; I suppose to be of some use after all.

It was then I discovered the glue: small, hard ice-piles of congealed glue scattered everywhere—as if some fantastic snowbeast had invaded the flat, dropping one confection after another of glueturds.

I think that I began to understand more than what I was seeing. There is a furious energy in what she is doing. I feel it now. She is emptying herself, can you imagine turning a body inside out?

Lately, she insists on telling me her dreams; a rare privilege and I listen patiently to her.

She begins by picking over one fragment then another; sorting through beginnings and endings, how admirably she is able to elaborate on middle passages, not at all hesitant about a puzzle of parts.

She tells them well. I hear: that she wants to be restoryed. Sometimes there are even snatches of songs, filling the gaps with anecdotes to prolong my attention, or provoke my open admiration. Once she danced the dream of just waking up, ending with the words: *What do you do when you have just finished putting your head into heaven?*

Gradually, we are beginning to turn the corner.

Only yesterday she began the day by inspecting the heels of a new pair of shoes I had bought from a shop on my way home the night before. You could smell the new, uncreased leather even through the shoebox lid.

Stiffening—she held them out at arm's length, the soles turned upward; points of light bouncing off the finely polished leather. And she showed me what I had never noticed before: the imprint of the lot number, 666. It may even have been the signature of a shopworker.

Suddenly—I was afraid that she might fall violently to the floor. She rolled her eyes back into her head, grinding her teeth, I could hear her just then gasping for air, repeating over and over, *just what you might expect, just what you might expect, after all, just what you might expect . . .*

And then, she just as suddenly fell into a deep sleep; she slept soundly for some time her head cradled in her arms on the table.

Finally, this morning she declared that after all she was determined to *carry out a raid against the unspeakable, even if there is no turning back, and amen.*

She spoke quite clearly, even calmly, almost I thought cheerfully, reading from a torn patch of notepaper held in the palm of her hand.

You will understand how much I was relieved. You can see there is simply no room left in the flat that hasn't been bandaged in newsprint.

Then she asked me would I care to step up to the window?

Yellow Chairs with Canary
1985

I would.

I could hear it at once—humming out there on the streets.

It seemed constant and everywhere in the air, and not unpleasant.

She held my arm lightly at the elbow guiding my sight. Looking out as I did just above the great dome, I could see: a large, smoke-coloured ball.

Imagine my surprise, when I began to notice how the globe was turning on its axis, growing larger and larger as it continued falling slowly into the city.

At that moment, despite the darkening of the sky as the sun began to slide away, I saw for the very first time on the face of the turning globe, the milky contours of what looked like all the continents of the earth.

And I saw, but only for a fleeting moment, still clearly I saw the figure of Marianina above the smoke-coloured globe.

She was levitating in a shock of blue light.

ROWLEY HABIB

Rowley Habib (b.1935) is of Ngati Tuwharetoa and Lebanese descent. He is a poet, short story writer, playwright and scriptwriter, whose 1974 television series 'Tihei Mauriora' dealt with aspects of Maori culture, past and present, and whose television play The Protesters *won a 1982 Feltex Script Award. His work is widely published in anthologies, and in translation in New Zealand and overseas.*

Menton Vignette I

Came the morning
And in the boat harbour below
all the riggings of the masts
set in mad motion by the gale
hit against the hollow
poles, setting up a wail
    As if some alien sound
    was in the air all round
    trying to be found
from the forgotten pasts
(Or the unknown future?)
of a wonderful orchestra
    giving due warning
    of an old time dawning
    (Or a new time spawning?)
awaiting the ageing maestro
with enthusiastic gusto
was tuning fantastic instruments
with counter-clashing compliments
and giving original birth
to a sound not of this Earth.

Menton Vignette III

What purpose, I wonder, that you'll find
One such of every preacher's kind
In any town of affluence
Where people of much influence
Gather to squander away their wealth
In search of happiness and health?
Is it an act of Providence
Come to prick the confidence
Of those who all their days have spent
Accumulating accoutrement?
For you'll see him when day begins
A manifestation of our sins
Shuffling his strickened ragged way
Through the pattern of our day
Like a biblical apparition
Scorning to shame the human condition
Or sleeping heapedly by a ditch
Along the boulevards of the rich
Like John the Baptist of latter-day
Warning us that we've gone astray
From the paths of righteousness
Down the paths of selfishness.
Or else you'll find this broken man
Rummaging in a rubbish can
For food the rich have cast away
To sustain him through another day.
Or yet you'll see him humbly stand
A pitiful sight on the golden strand
With eyes that seem to accusingly gaze
On the deeds of our human ways
Inaudibly muttering words
To the uncaring passing herds.
Could it be that he is saying
From the path of God we're straying?
And that there will come a day
When we'll all return to clay?

What purpose, I wonder, that you'll find
One such of every preacher's kind
Where people gather to spend their wealth
In search of happiness and health?

On the Beach
1981

Could it be for the rich to see
Another side of their destiny?
And to warn us that our need
Is but a product of our greed?

Ozymandias Revisited

(*after visiting the Berlin Wall*)

I met a traveller from a foreign land
who said: A tall and ugly wall of stone
stands in the heart of a great city. And
near it, there's a waste and barren zone
which presence testifies that still the hand
that mocked and the heart that fed survive.
Whose sneer of cold command and wrinkled lip
stamped itself upon some million lives.
For in this place a man once ruled and said
I Ozymandias hold you in my grip
look upon my works with fear and dread.
Nothing there is remains except the wall
and the silence that speaks the thing unsaid.
Here lies the pride that comes before the fall.

RUSSELL HALEY

Russell Haley was born in England in 1934, emigrated to Australia in 1961, and to New Zealand in 1966. His work has appeared in a wide variety of literary journals and most major anthologies and includes poetry, short stories and novels. Among his publications are The Walled Garden *(poems),* Real Illusions *(short stories),* Beside Myself *(novel) and a biography of the painter Pat Hanly. While in Europe he read his work at Commonwealth Literature conferences in Venice, Nice and Aachen and discussed New Zealand fiction in Cologne and at the universities of Utrecht and Dundee. What follows is the text of a paper he read in Nice.*

In Katherine Mansfield's Shadow

Katherine Mansfield lived and wrote at the Villa Isola Bella in Garavan from September 1920 until May of the following year. The early months of her stay in what was then a leafy suburb of Menton were the most prolific. Before Christmas she had sent Middleton Murry 'The Young Girl', 'The Stranger', 'The Ladies' Maid' and 'Poison'; 'The Daughters of the Late Colonel' seems to have been written by New Year's Day.

In commemoration of her importance as a writer from New Zealand and of her time in Menton the Katherine Mansfield Fellowship was founded by Cecil and Celia Manson of Wellington. From the early 'seventies a selected author has come every year from our country to write at the Isola Bella. The town of Menton provides us with a room below the terrace of the villa but the administration insists that we live elsewhere; the room is only a study.

One curious aspect of the Fellowship is that few of our writers appear to have been overtly influenced by the fact that Mansfield lived in the Isola Bella. However, what follows is merely an informal survey based on texts I brought with me and those left by previous occupants of the study.

And I admit that it is impossible to hear Mansfield's voice at the villa except by a large effort of the imagination. She once became exasperated with Marie, her housekeeper, who thought that *chou-fleur* were too expensive. Mansfield cried, 'Let us have a cauliflower at any price,' but I have only been able to hear that demand in my mind.

Yet the palm tree with leaves like feathers is still growing outside her bedroom window. Mansfield sat in the sun on the terrace just a few feet above where the Fellows now work. The mimosa is still there between the front doors and the gate even if it has been savagely pruned.

Of course there is no obligation to acknowledge even the faintest presence of Katherine

Mansfield in our writing, though Margaret Scott and C.K. Stead came to Menton with editorial projects which were related directly to Mansfield's papers.

But our fiction writers appear to have worked without K.M. looking over their shoulders. Michael Gifkins wrote a short story titled 'Summer is the Côte d'Azur' which has Menton as its setting and where the *Rainbow Warrior* bombing and the town's pampered dogs create difficulties for the main character.

Marilyn Duckworth features the town in a recent novel, *Rest for the Wicked*, but I believe that K.M. is absent from those pages. Mansfield does appear briefly in a poem by the same author when she writes of sharing 'Katherine's Room' with her sister, Fleur Adcock.

Janet Frame is one of the most distinguished New Zealand writers to have held the Fellowship. Mansfield appears obliquely in *Living in the Maniototo* in the guise of Margaret Rose Hurndell but this character is only referred to; Frame devotes more words to describing the study at the Isola Bella.

Rore Hapipi [Rowley Habib] had the Fellowship in 1984 and returned to Menton in 1987. When we talked it was obvious that he had immersed himself in Mansfield's writing and he helped me to 'place' her in Garavan. She may be a presence in his work but I haven't had the opportunity yet to read his latest fiction.

It happens that the most tangible evidence which I have found that Mansfield continues to inhabit our fiction is in the work of a novelist who has yet to be given the Fellowship. In Ian Wedde's *Symmes Hole* Kathleen 'comes back' and we discover her at a literary reception at the Beehive. Her presence is underscored by Wedde's reiteration of a Mansfield phrase from 'Prelude' where the Picton boat is 'all hung with bright beads' and lines from her letters enter the consciousness of an unnamed character: 'I shall remember every little thing about you forever.'

Other writers from other countries come knocking on the door of the study at the Isola Bella in search of Katherine Mansfield. Christa Moog of West Berlin has followed K.M. around Europe and New Zealand. She has written a novel about her responses to Mansfield and the places where she lived.

However, this brief glance at the work of a few of my predecessors is obviously quite inadequate. In the stories I have written at the Isola Bella there are no overt signs of Mansfield's presence or influence. The setting for my new fictions is Auckland's west coast and they are informed, I believe, by a similar impulse which drove Mansfield to write about New Zealand in many of her final stories from Menton in France and Montana in Switzerland. What follows, then, is a token payment for the debt I owe Katherine Mansfield—a debt which otherwise might not be perceived.

In a letter to Middleton Murry, Katherine Mansfield wrote that there were three large *caves* in the grounds of the Isola Bella. We can safely assume that Mansfield did not write in them and that they have been converted into the present study. So the Fellows work in Katherine Mansfield's cellar.

For me there have been positive advantages in writing 'underground'. Years ago I became interested in Gaston Bachelard's notion that the house, a structure in space, can be seen as an image of the psyche. It was certainly in the cellar/study/unconscious of the Isola Bella that I began to fully apprehend Mansfield's dreams.

When I came to Menton last September as the 1987 Fellow I already knew Mansfield's stories and I had read Alpers' biography. The *Journal* was new to me and so too were her letters. I did not know then that as I tried to write in the study my responses to her life, her work, and her dreams would deepen almost to the point of obsession yet I spent months at the Isola Bella before I faced what Mansfield and I really have in common.

Some of Katherine Mansfield's stories came to her in dreams. 'Sun and Moon' was one and 'The Young Girl', written in Menton, was, as she wrote to her husband, another of her 'queer hallucinations'.

Here is the closing sequence of a dream which Mansfield had in her pale yellow house. I am quoting this passage from her *Journal* because it seems to belong to us both. In my universe, where the dead cannot speak to us except in our dreams and fictions, Mansfield's ash is still falling.

She went to a Restoration play at a theatre in Piccadilly Circus but the actors began to speak too slowly, they drifted off stage, and a black iron curtain was lowered.

'An enormous crowd filled the Circus: it was black with people. They were not speaking— a low murmur came from it—that was all. They were still. A white-faced man looked over his shoulder and *trying to smile* he said: "The Heavens are changing already; there are six moons!"

'Then I realised that *our* earth had come to an end. I looked up. The sky was ashy-green; six livid quarters swam in it. A very fine soft ash began to fall. The crowd parted. A cart drawn by two small black horses appeared. Inside there were Salvation Army women doling tracts out of huge marked boxes. They gave me one! "Are you corrupted?"

'It got very dark and quiet and the ash fell faster. Nobody moved.'

These images of a *Restoration* play ending with mumbles and a descending iron curtain, silence and stillness, the funereal horses drawing a *Salvation* cart, and the question, 'Are you corrupted?' scarcely require interpretation. Nothing will be restored and salvation is dubious; Mansfield is dreaming about death.

This vision of ash and endings is, however, only one of the many stages Katherine Mansfield underwent in the recognition of her own death. An earlier and conscious realisation had occurred at Bandol in 1915.

That year her brother, Leslie Heron Beauchamp, had been killed in France when a faulty grenade exploded in his hand. In a *Journal* entry Mansfield explicitly linked her death to his: 'I think I have known for a long time that life was over for me, but I never realised it or acknowledged it until my brother died.'

This awareness that she was connected in death with her brother becomes even more apparent when we examine an unfinished story which Mansfield wrote in 1921 at the Chalet des Sapins.

In 'Six Years After' a woman in frail health is on a sea voyage with her husband. Out on deck she senses the presence of her son who was killed six years before in the war. She remembers a nightmare he had as a child: 'I dreamed I was in a wood—somewhere far away from everybody—and I was lying down and a great blackberry vine grew over me.' When Mansfield wrote in her *Journal* about her brother's grave she said he was 'lying in the middle of a little wood in France.'

The woman in the story is partly Mansfield's mother and partly herself but it is Katherine Mansfield's dream from the Isola Bella which finally occludes the story. These words occur abruptly: '. . . But softly without a sound the dark curtain has rolled down. There is no more to come. That is the end of the play.' There are four more short paragraphs and the penultimate one has this sentence: 'It is colder than ever, and now the dusk is falling, falling like ash upon the pallid water.'

The bond in life and in death between Katherine Mansfield and Leslie Beauchamp helps us to comprehend the terrifyingly flat statement she made in her *Journal* at Ospedaletti. Mansfield had a dream where her whole body broke up like glass and she wrote: 'I am (December 15, 1919) a dead woman, and *I don't care.*'

An understanding such as that cannot be forgotten, cannot be ignored. The knowledge flows back into the life through dreams and even when consciously described, as in a letter to Middleton Murry from the Isola Bella, the images selected seem to draw on archetypal strengths. Here, Katherine Mansfield writes of her death to her husband but we are almost with Charon, crossing the first river of Hell: 'We resist, we are terribly frightened. The little boat enters the dark fearful gulf and our only cry is to escape—"put me on land again". But it's useless. Nobody listens. The shadowy figure rows on. One ought to sit still and uncover one's eyes.'

That vision of the little ship of death dates from October, 1920, but I can't help feeling that Linda Burnell has a similar intuition when she looks at the aloe in 'Prelude'. That strange plant becomes a boat.

'She dreamed that she was caught up out of the cold water into the ship with the lifted oars and the budding mast. Now the oars fell striking quickly, quickly. They rowed far away over the top of the garden trees, the paddocks and the dark bush beyond. Ah, she heard herself cry: "Faster! Faster!" to those who were rowing.'

Linda, in her imagination, is escaping from Stanley Burnell and what is apparent if we compare 'Prelude' of 1917 with its predecessor 'The Aloe', written in 1915, is that the positive aspects of the 'ship' disappear in the later version. Mrs Fairfield thinks that if the aloe flowers it would be 'wonderfully lucky' in the 1915 text but in 'Prelude', composed two years later, that line was dropped.

But I must return now to Bandol in 1915 and complete Mansfield's *Journal* entry where she wrote of her death and that of her brother. She continued: 'Then why don't I commit suicide? Because I feel I have a duty to perform to the lovely time when we were both alive.'

That duty was, of course, to write the New Zealand stories which we now consider her greatest achievement. She was even more explicit, early in 1916, about what she had to do.

'Yes, I want to write about my own country till I simply exhaust my store. Not only because it is "a sacred debt" that I pay to my country because my brother and I were born there, but also because in my thoughts I range with him over all the remembered places.'

What we might have expected then from the last stories—a restoration of that 'lovely time' and 'remembered places'—does not fully correspond with our reading of them. I suggested earlier that Mansfield's Ospedaletti knowledge of death pervaded her remaining life and work and even a superficial glance at those final stories, as this must be, informs us that death is central to many of them.

In 'The Stranger' a husband is cuckolded, in a sense, by a dying traveller. A man has died in Mrs Hammond's arms as she returns from an overseas visit and the final line indicates how their marriage has been radically changed: 'They would never be alone together again.'

The businessman in 'The Fly' intends to weep for his son killed six years previously in the war but he occupies himself by drowning a fly in ink. In this appalling game the father forgets but *our* awareness of the son's death is intensified.

The Picnic
1991

A death finally shrouds the gaiety of 'The Garden Party' and in 'The Voyage' Fenella is catching the Picton boat, 'all beaded with round golden lights,' because her mother has died.

A wife is poisoned, it seems, in the unfinished 'A Married Man's Story' and the after-effects of a death are felt in 'The Daughters of the Late Colonel'.

This too swift summary should not, I hope, obscure my admiration for Mansfield's final stories and she does write superbly of 'lovely times' in 'At the Bay'. I am suggesting, however, that the death theme is not only important in the stories Mansfield wrote at the Isola Bella and in Montana—it is inevitable.

I want to come back now to my relationship with Mansfield's life and work and to make any sense of what I have already said I must refer to a note which she scribbled in her diary when Mansfield first came to Menton from Ospedaletti. She had crossed more than one frontier: 'At the back of my mind I am so wretched. But all the while I am thinking over my philosophy—the defeat of the personal.'

Those last five words have, apparently, caused some puzzlement. They were written in pencil and are almost illegible. Anthony Alpers poses the question: 'What *did* she mean?' A page later in the *Life* he asks again: 'Defeat or conquest? Failure admitted, or challenge accepted?'

I believe that the answer rests in Mansfield's final stories. There is nothing more personal than death and we only defeat it by accepting it. We are driven towards paradox; death *illuminates* many of her last stories. She *knew* she was dead and she defeated that personal fact in her writing.

When I read those words: 'I am a dead woman, and *I don't care*' I understood precisely what Katherine Mansfield meant. She spoke directly to me. But I was defeated in a different way. I was *not* writing. I had produced one short story in two years. My silence stemmed from a realisation similar to the one Mansfield had in Bandol in 1915—that we die through the death of another.

In March, 1986, our daughter was killed in an accident on Auckland's north-western motorway. Her name was Katherine. I knew then that I was also dead. Like Mansfield I too *did not care*.

Yet the fact remains that Katherine Mansfield kept on writing. It is what she did with courage, what she *did* with all her deaths, which enabled me to move on and I owe her that debt.

For months in that underground room at the Villa Isola Bella I was willingly in Katherine Mansfield's shadow. And having gone through her deaths, dreaming her dreams, finally accepting my own deaths, I emerged from the shadows in January and began to write my own stories.

Villa Isola Bella
March, 1988

JANET FRAME

Janet Frame (b.1924) is New Zealand's most distinguished novelist, a reputation earned over forty years and more than fifteen books, including Scented Gardens for the Blind, Living in the Maniototo *and* The Carpathians. *Her work has won many prizes and she has been awarded an OBE, an honorary LittD from the University of Otago, and is an honorary foreign member of the American Academy of Arts and Letters. The three volumes of her autobiography have been made into the feature film* An Angel at my Table.

From Living in the Maniototo

And I thought of the room in Menton in the villa where Margaret Rose Hurndell had lived, and how I had visited the room. I walked up a narrow street beneath a railway bridge and up another street that had once been a Roman Road, and on the left I saw the plaque, *Margaret Rose Hurndell Memorial Room*, giving the date of her birth and death (born 1930—the same year as the Princess Margaret Rose—died in 1957; and like Peter Wallstead largely unknown until after her death) and a list of her writings. The garden was overgrown with weeds, the stairs leading to the small room were thick with sodden leaves and fragments of paper thrown off the street. I put the Margaret Rose Hurndell Key (which I had borrowed) in the lock and pushed open the sun-blistered wooden door which permitted itself to open halfway: it has 'dropped' like an old used womb. I walked in. I opened the tiny windows, pushing back the branches that crowded against them. The room slowly became 'aired' like old stored linen. Small chutchutting birds with whistlings and secretive noises began stirring outside. A cool wind blew through the windows and out the door, a between-winter-and-spring wind. There was an air of desolation in the room and beyond it. A water-spotted plaque inside gave further details of Margaret Rose Hurndell's career. There were a few straight-backed vicarage-type chairs in the room, and a desk and a bookshelf (an Armstrong Fellow came each year to work in the memorial room); and layers of cold along the bare, tiled floor. I could hear the grass swaying in the neglected garden, and the brittle rustling of the flax bush, now a mass of soaring green spears, which a sympathetic writer had planted near the crumbling wall.

Here, I thought, if one were a spirit or dead, is a sanctuary. With a sudden rush of wind, dead leaves, twigs and a scrap of paper blew inside. The air of desolation and neglect increased: the chill, of the wind and of the spirit, intensified and there was the kind of peace that one feels walking among the dead and listening, as the dead may, at a great distance from the world and

The Garden
1990

its movement and noise.

I went to explore the small garden and found a green garden seat which I cleared, brushing away the bruised ripe loquats fallen everywhere from the huge loquat tree; and I lay down, half in sun, half in shadow, looking up at the lemon tree in the neighbouring garden of the Villa Florita. I closed my eyes. The sun came out again, moving quickly, and was on my face, burning. I changed my position on the seat. The sun was once again hidden behind cloud, the air was chill again, the flax rustled with a brittle snapping sound and the secretive small birds once again began their whispering and chittering. I fell asleep. And when I woke I shivered with cold. The mountains were harsh and grey with fallen used daylight, softened in the crevices with the blue of distance and evening.

So that was the Rose Hurndell Room!

LAURIS EDMOND

Lauris Edmond (b.1924) has published nine volumes of poetry, including Salt from the North: Poems *and* Summer near the Arctic Circle. *Her* Selected Poems *won the Commonwealth Poetry Prize in 1985. She has also written a novel and three volumes of an autobiography.*

From The Quick World

April 18: Easter Saturday. I wake to the sound of rain; if this is the best climate in the world it rains surprisingly often. Not that I mind—it always brings a delicious freshness with it. Madame Raynaud with whom I am to lunch arrives at 10 a.m., bringing me a crocheted shawl as an Easter present. Then we walk, slowly, since though spry she is very old, to the other end of town where she has an apartment in one of the huge 19th-century palaces whose sweeping staircases and marble pillars are now thoroughfares for hundreds of tenants. Madame belongs to a family that traces its ancestry back to Joan of Arc; her husband, who died recently, was a colonel in the French army. Naturally her opinions are unshakeably conservative, but her manner while she dismisses unsuitable persons or practices is urbane, her conversation witty and stylish. Her English, which she learned in childhood from a governess, is excellent.

She lived for ten years in Romania and tells me that the Romanians are charming but have no morals whatever. They change partners, they marry and re-marry, they have a different father for every child in the family. When you ask a Romanian woman to sit down, she lies down, it's what she thinks you mean. When Madame left she was complimented on having remained happily married and caused no scandal. It is because I have *l'équilibre*, she says; that is what one needs.

Simone de Beauvoir is mentioned. Madame has no time for her. Sartre? Worse. He caused nothing but trouble. She talks of the church, has several nephews who are priests. Celibacy? it is a practical matter; there is the expense of supporting wives and children—a priest is always poor. More important, he holds the secrets of the confessional; if he were married he would tell them to his wife and then everyone would know. Only if confession were abolished could priests marry. However, she adds, many in France are married because they come to the priesthood from other professions. Do they keep their wives? Well of course. We are not careless.

Nor are they dirty and untidy like the Italians and the English who are absent-minded as well, and terrible gossips. Indeed, it seems there are no other races that measure up. The Russians are morose, the Swedes drink too much—everyone is drunk in Sweden; if you sit down in a public square in Stockholm a policeman comes and shakes you because he knows you must be drunk and he wants to know what you're thinking of doing. And the Central Europeans, the Croats, Serbs, Bohemians, Bulgarians and the rest—they are all like the Romanians, entirely without morals. The trouble is the Greek Orthodox Church, it allows anything, has no standards, no rules. People think this about the French but it's not true; they are a very formal people with a great respect for their institutions. When Monsieur was in a German prison camp during the war Madame worked in an American canteen; as soon as the men knew you were French they would begin shouting 'coucher! coucher!' at you. The very idea . . . she is full of scorn.

It is all delightful. Before I leave I learn too that there are hotels in the town to which one must never send one's friends because they are fit only for those particularly despicable creatures, the English railway crowd. Also that the English postal service is so complicated that every postman has to stay in the same job for the whole of his life, because no one can learn it twice. She sees that I am enjoying her prejudices, and of course enjoys them a good deal herself. We will meet again; she will take me to a concert in the Chapelle des Pénitents Noirs, there is a fine local flautist whom I must hear. When I leave I am permitted the French kiss on both cheeks, and a final piece of instruction. Some vulgar people overdo this salutation—they do it twice on each cheek, without expression, without enthusiasm; you can tell they come from the lower classes.

April 19: I was to go to Mme Bosano's for lunch and of course missed all my buses and connections and in the end walked all the way, miles from here, on the other side of town. It's a country road really—I walked up the quietest stretches, so hushed I hardly dared to let my foot make a sound in the silence and under those enormous trees, feathery and delicate far above my head. Elms and oaks, a few pines, shedding a secret, soundless floor where I walked.

And then suddenly, I was there, up some steps to a side door, which opened as though someone had been watching for me and at once I was looking at a large photo of a tabby cat. Dressed, with a tiny bow tie, the gentleman who had been so downcast the day I came and found him in his dressing gown, presented it—he'd been waiting to receive me into what looked like his study, sprang from behind the curtains with a sort of mute *bonjour*. I imagine he needs that room to escape from the ebullience of Madame. We went through hundreds of photos—Paris in wartime, Paris in winter, their children and everyone else's, chateaux and cathedrals. He told me how to correct the distortion of a photo of something high above you; he was sweet and gentle and I could talk French to him easily.

No sign of Madame, time went on and on; far too polite to voice my questions, I sat on admiring every single item in his collection when Boom! Boom! in bursts Madame. He hadn't told her I was there! Fancy! And I was! She'd been wondering what to do about me. At once the gentle monsieur put his photos away and assumed the humble mien I'd seen before; he would hardly raise his head, he couldn't. We followed Madame like naughty children, upstairs and into an austerely charming living room with windows on all sides and views of mountains and valleys from every one. I was utterly delighted. But there wasn't time to meditate and explain—business! In other words, food! Mme disappeared briefly and Monsieur invited me to sign their Livre d'Or where all their friends are. I was ashamed not to be able to add my compliments to those I read, but really—what could I say? Have just arrived, saw photographs, expect to have a marvellous time. I signed my name. The food was perfect, from the tomato and olive pizza and veal and mushrooms to the tiny biscuits like baby brandy snaps called Cigarettes Russes, the wine, a good burgundy, coffee . . . Then we staggered out, Madame and I, because she decided to take me to visit some people who walk. WALK! (really she is wearing after a while). The people were delightful, spoke not a word of English, but explained perfectly well what I must do to walk next day. I was reluctant, too busy, je dois travailler . . . Oh non! non! Easter Monday is a holiday, nobody must work. *Heureux pacques* . . . So of course I agreed. We had to drink some strong hot coffee and were offered biscuits, which I refused—but Madame took one, broke half off and gave it to me, quite as though (again) I was a child who had failed to mind its manners. I was half amused, half cross, but our hosts were pleased with everything; gave us some red rose buds from a wonderful crimson curtain of them hanging on a fence, and at last let us go.

Now I could go home. But no, Madame has another plan—we are to go to Mme Rouvel's because there is a person there I must meet, and, since she lives near me, will take me home. I am in her toils. We go. The person turns out to be another ancient lady who is coquettish about admitting she can speak any English. Oh naughty naughty! All of them become skittish, they poke fun, they roll about with laughter. It is awful. The clock says four and I'd been promised I could be home by three (not that it matters exactly, except that for once home is a refuge)—but—we've had no tea! Of course—I've lost all hope. The tea wagon appears, there is a plate of tiny cakes; Madame (mine) positively squeals with joy and desire. She is to be tempted. She must not! She is going to succumb, and feels it! Not wanting to invite another public correction I take the smallest I can see and push it down into my already overstuffed inside. But that is not enough—they are passed again. No thank you. No, really, delicious, but . . . She returns not once but twice more, the little ogre (she's about four feet high) and positively forces another into my hand, down my throat.

I don't know when we left. Five o'clock? Five-thirty? I had given up all hope and didn't even try to understand the shrieked anecdotes at which they were all doubled up. Finally Madame dropped us—me and the coquettish old thing—and then she insisted I go to her place. I was nearly crying with impatience, but she held me with her hand on my arm till I agreed. Mercifully I didn't have to go up to her floor, just make sure I knew how to call on her. She was to have the other ladies *mardi*—in two days' time? NO! I wouldn't, I would be working—at least I managed that. When I got home I sat down and fell instantly into an exhausted (and no doubt overfed) slumber. I hope never to see another elderly Frenchwoman as long as I live.

I like the French—today, at least. Along the waterfront boulevards there are couples walking at all hours of the day and night, men and women of all ages, together and at ease in a way I think is rare in New Zealand. They neither ignore nor overly concentrate on each other, they simply behave—walking, sitting, eating and drinking, shopping—in a way that makes being together wholly natural. As natural as being alone, yet more sustaining. More often than not they link arms or hold hands; there is something very touching about two of the very old wandering along hand in hand—but none of them are conscious of it in the way we would be. The local supermarket emblem is a couple holding a basket between them.

Of course many are retired people. There is too the different organisation of the day; there's a morning which starts early and ends at 12 or 12.30, lunch time, when only the restaurants are open and everyone falls to with great seriousness; and the afternoon which begins at 2.30 or 3 and may last till 7.30 or 8 in the evening. After that there's the promenade. Dogs take part in it too. There are nine million dogs in France and I am convinced that eight and a half million of them live in Menton. All are on leads, all docile, as decorous as their owners, except that they shit in the street.

Sometimes I have a desperate longing to see an animal running free or a tree, unpruned, growing wild and spreading itself copiously about the sky, or even an untended garden. Then I walk across the border into Italy. At once the paths are cracked, the geraniums and arctotis sprawl, passers-by greet you like amiable villagers; the beaches, unimproved, are rough and beset by rocks, bottles lie in enormous piles under stone arches that support the railway line.

April 20: Well, I went, I walked. Four or five hours' climbing on well-surfaced tracks to cols, peaks, saddles, up and down slopes. Lovely country with its open, cool, wraith-like forest, very airy and delicate—it's still early spring up there and the leaves were hardly uncurled—and the floor a mass of wild flowers, violets, primroses, pennyroyal, wild strawberries and a dozen different herbs. We sat down to rest and eat on stone remains of wartime fortifications or on the smooth white boulders that lie everywhere. A mist blew across the peaks—a strange, legendary landscape, the mountains and forests of fairy tale. It's almost like a racial memory, the feeling of recognition I have here at times. Perhaps it is that. Some of the steep slopes below us were still marked with the terraces on which grew the fruit and vegetables that fed the Roman armies. They were used for centuries afterwards, most recently to feed the tourists when the coastal towns became fashionable in the 19th century. But no more—the grass has grown over them and packaged refrigerated foods, mass produced on more accessible ground, are brought in from other parts of France and Italy.

We drove down through a violent thunderstorm and the English teacher (that is, the French teacher of English) who brought me home told me she lives by the week in Cannes where she works; would I like to stay with her during the Cannes Film Festival? Would I!

May 2: This morning there was a minor catastrophe. I was sitting out on the seat, cooking quietly in the sun, rolling along through a scene with my stones nearby to keep each pile from shifting in the wind (no, wind never blows in this secluded corner, a faint lifting of the air). One for the finished pages, one for the outline of the section in case I needed it, one for the notes on N who has been slipping out of gear the last few days. A car drew up at the gate and out stepped not just an example of the type of the 19th-century English—the originals. Two ladies. Complacent, patronising, voluble on small matters; adored the climate but clearly despised the French—pronounced Garavan as though it's caravan, and they've lived here eight years. Would I come for a drink on Thursday? Usually it's tea at 4.30 and I must say a drink was tempting; anyway I never refuse the first time. They sat beside me (I'd hastily removed my rock-crowned heaps) covered in their dark, leathery, over-exposed skins, looking as though they were more than half reptile (will I look like this after a Riviera summer?) and held forth about the price of whisky. I don't like it much whatever it costs, but that hardly added to the general irrelevance.

After they'd gone I was furious—with them, with myself for not knowing how to get rid of them, with the world in general that it hangs by so slim a thread. It's true, it does. Often in the afternoons when I'm not struggling with *Weather* I am forlorn, especially if it's been a day without much mail. If there isn't any at all I allow myself a gin and tonic before lunch (someone's given me a fridge); if there's a pile, I sometimes go down to the corner and lunch at 'Les Folies' and am served solemnly and ceremoniously by la grosse Madame while I read it. It's quite a cheap celebration—the plat du jour is only 27 francs and it's always delicious. The French don't know how to cook badly. Then I come home and write letters or type the morning's work or read or go walking, or go out if I've been asked.

May 10: Mitterrand is in! And by a huge 4%—it's a landslide. I can scarcely believe it, Giscard seemed so entrenched. The only hopeful sign I saw was the other day, a bunch of bankers and industrialists who were on the Socialists' list for nationalisation were asked what they thought about it, and they all said 'no comment'—as though they expected Mitterrand to win. There was a thunderstorm tonight, and even though this is, of course, a blue-ribbon district there were some gunshots and rockets not far away from me about nine o'clock. The radio says the people danced on the Bastille in the rain. What a time to be in France! Bliss was it in that dawn . . . it really feels like that. He's been talking heroically about the French people and la République in the last weeks, and I don't think it's just rhetoric. But when a journalist asked him tonight what he'd do first tomorrow he said, 'Get up, same as every other morning.' I thought that was nice.

Madame Raynaud came to see me this morning after she'd voted (for Giscard, I bet, but we didn't discuss it). She has another crime to add to those committed by the English. They take the combings out of their hair brushes and roll them round their fingers and then put them carefully in a drawer! She's seen them do it. Oh I love her—she's superb.

May 22: I've been to Cannes. Wonderful to be able to say it, and wonderful in truth it was. Those good films . . . all that unexpected national pride . . . that glittering crowd. Being among those other New Zealanders did something strange—it lifted off the weight of solitude like the peeling off of one heavy garment after another on a hot day. Now I'm back I have an almost physical sense of turning inwards again. I have waved goodbye, smiling brightly, I turn at the door, I begin the concentration that will slowly bring up the outline of my own mental furniture. It's like learning—or waiting to be able—to see in the dark.

But coming home was a special thing in another way. For the very first time my little house actually represented home (I don't count the initial euphoria when I rhapsodised about it being mine, mine, tra la) and I came to it with keen pleasure. The datura was covered with richly scented trumpets, there were passionfruit flowers, exquisite as orchids, all over the vine on the fence—and at least a thousand letters from New Zealand in my mail box.

. . . Last night I had dinner with a girl from the Paris Embassy who's here; she's cheerful and talkative, wonderfully convincing as a New Zealander. Coming home along the Promenade de la Mer at about 10.30 I was followed by a dark young man, an Algerian I suppose. He spoke to me in several languages, or mixtures thereof, and would not go away. Finally, quite considerably frightened, I crossed to the other side of the street and walked fast, seeing another person, helpful I hoped, in the distance. He proved to be a reassuringly middle-aged man and when I gasped at him, Demandez à ce jeune homme de laisser moi (of doubtful accuracy, but the point was clear), the dear creature took my hand in a friendly fashion and said But you know me! And I did—he's an Englishman who'd called one day and left his card and invited me to visit him and his Italian wife; he's a translator for some firm in Monte Carlo. He shook my young man off and walked me home, very companionably. Now I'll have to go and visit him, out of gratitude.

Last evening I was walking up under my stone railway bridge about six o'clock when a car stopped and two women called out to me. One was Mme Raynaud, who has infinite ingenuity and arrives with a different person every time. The driver turned out to be Mary-Adèle, referred to by everyone as the Friend of the Fellow. She's American-French, very bright and friendly; doesn't listen; but anyway we're to go to her house for tea.

It's miles and miles up in the hills above Rocquebrune, with a breathtaking view of the Mediterranean; a cold, characterless house full of marble and white surfaces and ugly furniture and ornate decorations, like a huge bronze family group sculpture. Her American husband was all charm and superficiality too, took me out to admire the view and kept saying behind his hand that there was nothing wrong with France except the French. He drank whisky but the rest of us had tea out of a hideous curly black and green teaset—like the house, ornate and vulgar. I'm sure they have millions. Conversation that was constantly full of promise but constantly died. Whenever that happened John, the husband, would say Well now, we were talking about dogs, and the time it takes to travel to Australia . . . and we'd rouse ourselves and try again. And all the time there was the brilliant blue of the Mediterranean framed by marble pillars; it was like being in a rather badly rehearsed film.

As we left to come home—she would drive us home of course—two of her children appeared to greet Madame and be introduced to me. When Mary-Adèle said to the girl (as she had already said to the husband), 'Do take the meat loaf out of the freezer so it's not too cold for us to eat', the girl looked utterly disgusted and said several times, 'Don't say there's no food to eat again!' but her mother kept smiling and talking and ignored her. Strange lives, the rich live. I asked her—the mother—if she spent six months of the year in Menton and six months in New Orleans. Ah no, if only she could, it would be so simple—actually she spent most of the year in a jet plane somewhere across the Atlantic. Perhaps it's not so bad to have to save like mad for a single fare to go anywhere.

Now they've begun, there's no end to my remarkable experiences. The woman I must meet who is said to be literary (it turned out she'd once had T.S. Eliot to tea); two terrible English ladies, one fat one thin—Knife and Spoon— who drank their tea noisily and thirstily (not like the French who treat it as the poison it is, when they make it) and discoursed for an hour about how disgraceful it is that nobody in England speaks English any more—and then couldn't pronounce Salle des Variétés and had to point it out to each other on a brochure. And Yvette, the plump and personable widow who told me how at a young age (forty-five? more, probably) she had made herself rise above her grief at her husband's death and carry out alone their cherished scheme, to live beautifully in Menton. C'est une femme courageuse, everyone says—and how smiling and well-fleshed it has made her; I was taken over the apartment, furnished to the last degree—I mean, while you're there you can think of nothing but the furniture; those tightly stuffed little floral chairs, sitting up and folding their hands ready to take tea, those matching towels (lime green) in the bathroom, and the palest of twining green leaves creeping about on the wallpaper—living beautifully indeed.

In a town where a good part of the population declares it has come here to die, the cemetery has to be a major suburb. It is enormous, tier upon tier of concrete walls supporting broad terraces full of graves—and not just single ones; families. They die here as they have lived, behind locked gates that protect little courtyards from intruders or thieves. I think it's mainly the second they worry about, because there are statues and vases and other treasures left on the graves. It makes me think of the Egyptians.

That's the French and Italians; the English are, as one would expect, more discreet. Plain crosses and slabs for them, the excessiveness is in the inscriptions. Many speak for themselves of tragic deaths far from home—loved daughters of fifteen, nineteen, twenty-one, twenty-seven who 'died at Mentone'—as late as the twenties it was still called by the old Italian name. Many of the older English were distinguished and have insisted on carrying their honours into the next world—baronets, knights, colonels, majors, announce their rank. Dear me, the vanity—and all are becoming obliterated; some are already dusty relics under pine trees, the stones cracked and pine needles swept by the wind into piles that cover the names.

Now I've met a Radiant Living enthusiast—he's a sort of central guru for 'Amour et Lumière', an offshoot of Christian Science I think; laying yourself open to the perfection of the universe so you are in its stream, as it were, it enters you and your illnesses and woes are harmonised out of existence. How Fanny and Lewis would have liked it. I drank tea in his house, this ancient rather splendid Frenchman, and his English wife, then they took me for a walk among the colossal mansions in Cap Martin owned by absentee rich who keep them tended by a staff and come once a year to hold house parties. A silent lane, hushed with reverence for such grandeur; we tiptoe along it, then back for the usual tea of sweet cakes and terrible tea.

Then there was a thunderstorm, the sky darkened, and the room; they recovered from the desire to send me down the hill to catch a bus and decided to drive me home. I sat in the front with Monsieur and watched the spectacle—the sky purple and black over the old town, the sea marching up the beach like a charge of cavalry, and then the roar of the rain. Wonderful.

One thing living here teaches you is neither to envy the rich nor to be sorry for them. In the end money makes them boring, and it's their own fault. Of course there are exceptions—there's William, the only real Eton-and-Oxford man I've ever known, and an aristocrat. He's fun, and sharp-witted, and sometimes cranky, and lives in his great villa with its classic English garden as though it really is an occupation. He has grand relations and is a younger son—this is his fate, perhaps, to be 'sent out' (is that how they'd put it—as if to India or Australia?) to tend the family property. He says if I send him a pohutukawa seedling it might grow in their rather similar climate; he has a cypress walk, a lily pond, a stone wall incorporating someone's memorial stone; it's no wonder I often think I've entered the world of legend and childhood tales by coming here.

One day we went to St Agnès, one of the high mountain villages, zig-zagging up and up in the little bus. It's a cluster of medieval houses in the lee of one of the peaks; many of the streets were steps, going in and out of archways—one actually said ninth century, carved in the stone—more than a thousand years of the tramp of feet over these rounded cobblestones, and the great blue peaks of the mountains all around us moving in and out of the mist, as they must always have done, season after endless season . . .

June 7: A letter from the Paris Embassy asking me to go to lunch on the 12th. I can't possibly, I can't do any mortal thing till I've finished this draft of *Weather*. I'll write and explain. How many days are there? I wonder if I just write, night and day, from now till then and leave the typing till later, if I possibly could? Paris, for a weekend . . . It will kill me, but I don't suppose that matters.

June 9: I've finished! So many thousands of times I've thought it would just go on and on for

The Family Room
1991

ever—and now I've done it! I can't sleep, haven't slept properly for several nights, but I don't care, I don't care about anything except that it's DONE. And now, I even like it—I came to love them in the end, Nigel and Louise and the rest. Of course I may be quite wrong, everything may be a mess, but I don't think so. I began to feel all right when I learnt how to punish them, push them further, not just let them stand round and be pleased with themselves, which earlier they showed a tendency to do. I went to Italy and bought some shoes.

MAURICE GEE

Maurice Gee (b.1931) is the prizewinning author of ten novels,
including the acclaimed Plumb *trilogy,* Prowlers, The Burning Boy
and Going West; *two short story collections; and a number of novels*
for children including The Halfmen of O *and* The Fire-raiser. *He also*
writes extensively for television. 'Gwen Walks the Dog' *is an extract*
from a forthcoming novel with the working title of Crime Story.
'My novel is still rough and unrevised . . . In the end it seemed better
to settle for the first words I wrote in Menton. You'll see a Menton
influence—the dog shit. Already after three days here I was walking
with my eyes cast down. Apart from the story (not included here)
about the fellow in Monte Carlo who bought his favourite restaurant
to get a table and then gave it (the restaurant) to the waiter as a tip,
it's the only one I can identify in the whole book.'

Gwen Walks the Dog

The dog is half dachshund and half pug; a mix that denies it both intelligence and charm. Gwen Peet, who likes birds—free birds—lizards, weasels, possums, mice, and cats when independent, in descending order, and dogs hardly at all, is not able to be kind to the animal. Smelly, overfed, useless; tugging it along. She tugs when no one is looking. She drags it away from fences and hefts it up kerbs with her shoe. If it were left to her she would ban dogs from the streets, or make special neighbourhoods where they and their owners must live, and mark the boundaries with some dull dog-turdy colour or dog-turd sign, and fine anyone who stepped outside. Would Olivia go there, with her Butch, or would she choose people?

Gwen walks the dog each day as a favour to Olivia. Now and then she calls it a contribution. Grandma did this for me, she imagines the girl saying, and sees her slip each favour like a coin into her purse. She does not think of it as buying love. Contribution, necessary chore, like spooning Farex into her, not so long ago. She does not want love from Olivia, liking will do— for the reason, she agrees, that she does not love the girl herself, but merely likes, and liking is much to be preferred. It is nourishing and steady, while love is always too much or too little and makes one over-certain or uncertain, never sure.

So, the dog is a mongrel. And Gwen is a divorcee, not a wife. Although she can look younger she is sixty-four. She lives in the Kelburn house—not worth half a million, but $300,000 perhaps—her husband left her when he left. It's all she has apart from a small investment that earns enough for food and electricity and the rates. She has no car but rents her garage to a neighbour for $40 a week. She buys, when she has to, good clothes and shoes, because they last longer and work out cheaper in the end. Carefulness is something she has learned, it does not come naturally to her and she commits extravagances that don't reveal themselves at once but drive her to arithmetic when she cannot sleep in the night. Four a.m. is her bad time. The house creaks and the walls find new alignments and sets of figures move like draughts about the room. Curtains lift and stir in her mind. There's dark outside, no bright day, and past and future are alike, without significance. It sometimes helps her then to think that people she's attached to are next door, sleeping on a level with her—even if the filthy dog has left his basket for a place on Olivia's bed.

'Smelly thing,' she mutters, and touches its hind parts with her toe, making it scuttle out of range. 'Look at the funny wee doggy,' mothers will say; and children ask, 'What's your doggy's name?' 'Butch,' she replies, or, 'Four-legs, Yip-Yap, Greedy-Guts,' whatever comes to mind; and sometimes adds silently, Bad Smell, Pavement Pooper, Waste of Time. 'Don't touch him, he nips,' which is true. Butch has pinpricked chubby little fingers several times.

Gwen walks to the top of the cable car and round the bus roundabout and back to Central Terrace and so home every weekday, wet or fine, but doesn't go into the gardens because the dog spoils them. She walks there in the mornings and on cool late afternoons. She thinks about many things—money, food, the mountains, being alone, being further south, down where it snows, with nothing but grey oceans between her and Antarctica; and of a little house in the bush, up from Karamea perhaps, and no one there with her, not even a dog, just the birds and the river and the weather and the sky—lovely, she imagines, knowing it would suit her for a day or two; and thinks of people she has known, and knows but does not see for this reason or that, and those she does see and still enjoys, and those she can't get out of her life without causing pain. How many friends can a person have—half a dozen perhaps? And what can be done with the others, who knock against one, claiming, importuning?

She thinks of the future often; and of what Ulla calls her 'lot in life'. The two won't come apart. Her lot in life determines all the things that she will do. Oh no, she says, not everything, not all. There are so many freedoms she can claim—freedoms of the mind. There is nowhere she can't travel in there—except, she concedes, those places put off limits by race and gender; by language and by temperament; by prejudice, belief. Oh dear, dark continents, she thinks; but is not distressed because it is the same, or much the same, for everyone. It's still huge, it's limitless, the world outside her 'lot in life'.

All the same she thinks of that and of how it constrains her. Boundaries have been changed by her divorce but boundaries are not done away with. A huge natural feature is removed. The sun shines longer; at night more stars are in the sky; and she can stride on paths closed off before; but in the end day and night remain much as they were, just more of them, or less, and hotter, brighter, colder than before. Eating, sleeping, ageing still go on, and the house still creaks and the garden grows and prices rise and shoes wear out and Gwen Peet is altered here and there, but is recognisably the same. There are boundaries she still can't cross.

Howie said, 'Take it. You've earned it,' and meant no criticism of himself. It was, of course, already in her name, and she would have had it anyway. Her house. 'My house.' But let him think it lay within his gift. Too much energy would be spent in making him understand that he had never lived in it. And pleasure outweighed her bitterness. She made him a cup of coffee and put a little Scotch in—the last of his Scotch—and waited for him to become sentimental, and thought that his face was redder and fatter, all in a month, while his body was leaner,

Woman on Yellow Chaise Longue
1992

perhaps to facilitate new pleasures of the bed. Be careful Howie, she thought of saying, don't overdo things; but her happiness wouldn't allow it and she found herself thinking, Go for it, old boy, get in there.

He would, of course. All her men are greedy, Howard, Athol, Gordon; grabbers and getters. But Howie is a natural, born with a money scoop for a hand and a reach like a praying mantis, while his sons, her sons—it amazes her, men from her body—pause too often and think too much. She is afraid for them. She does not like them. Against her mature judgment, she still likes Howie. Being divorced from him is better than being married though. She can only define her new state by saying, Gwen Peet. 'Take your maiden name again,' some of her friends have insisted. But no, maiden will not do, maiden denies not affirms, and she is past such innocence. Peet is her because it takes her life in. Let Howie take a new name, he is the one who wants to put those years aside.

She turns in the roundabout, lets the dog pee, glances with amusement at tourists photographing the cable car; and distaste at the skull restaurant; then goes back towards Upland Road, past the doctors' rooms and the reassuringly scruffy seven-day dairy. The gallery comes next—these stations on her dutiful way—with new paintings in place, ugly and bright. Deliberately ugly? There is a lot of that about; and now and then she sees the point. Deliberately beautiful never has anything to say; or even show, when you get down to it. She does not tie the dog up and go in, has not sufficient strength of mind for glum women with shopping bags, and jowly Round Tablers are they, even in paint. She does not want to know about hungers and poverty, either of the body or mind, not just now. There are times for being angry and times for fear, and the air is fresh this morning, the wind lifting petrol fumes into the upper air. She does not want her easiness disturbed.

'Come on, mongrel,' she says, and crosses the road against the flow of students; climbs up, climbs down, into Central Terrace, and pauses for the distant mirror glass and the soaring cranes. The tallest of them stands on the site Howie had failed to secure; but he is busy down the Quay with another deal, a better site. There is always better, there is great—'good' never describes a project for it is tame. 'Best', too, has little use. It suggests an end and Howie and his mates mean to go on forever. One more time is built into them like a sense, and no more than an animal—no more than this dog snuffling in the puha, and surely within a year or two of pegging out—do they seem to have any sense of death. Or is that to assume too much? Do they, does Howie, have bad times at 4 a.m? Do the swinging cranes rust in their moving parts, the foundations fill with water and grow weeds, the mirror glass crack? It has all run down for Gordon, it has finished for the players who had failed to—what was it, dictate each event of the day to a secretary, and notarise it and put it in the lawyer's safe? Cover themselves. Howie had, Gordy hadn't. So the father is busy on the Quay, putting a new deal together, while the son sits in Auckland in a courtroom and hears the prosecution lawyers call him 'a man greedy to the very marrow of his bones'. It isn't true; Gordy is a dupe and not greedy in that way; but simply to be big, to be with the big boys, where his dad is, and not bright enough and quick enough and nowhere near long enough in the arm for it.

Not true, not fair, she says, but with no strength, for anger is educated out of her now and pity for Gordon is as much as she can feel. Pity for him, admiration for Howie, with some contempt; but for Athol anger, yes, anger and dislike. If she loved him a little more she would also hate him. If she loved him as she had done when he was a child . . .

Gwen unfastens the lead from Butch's collar. He is tired and will waddle along without leaving the footpath. She can go at her own pace and seem not to know him, and if the chain hanging from her fist gives her away she's not far enough ahead to make it seem she's unaware of his comfort stops. One day she'll come down with a bucket of hot water and Sunlight soap and a scrubbing brush and scrub the path clean—has not ruled it out as an eccentricity for her old age. Her seventies perhaps. Sixty-four can't get away with it; her mind still sharp, some few expectations still in place, rules to obey. Sons to nudge along and raise her voice against; Ulla to watch, Ulla to be eyes and ears for, and home and nation; Olivia, Damon: all these a consequence of Gwen and Howie meeting and marrying. They are now her lot in life, or a part of it. Not a part of Howie's, of course. Howie does not have a lot in life. He simply has opportunities. Down there a city block empties out, and down there a shining tower stands in Howie's mind, to take its place.

Yes, he dreams. Yes he has a vision of beauty. Athol does not have one. Gordy has some poor lopped-off thing. And she, Gwen? What she sees will not hold its shape, what she desires is multifarious. The university empties out its children. They hop and sidestep, dance and angle on Kelburn Parade and behave no differently from the boys and girls of her day there; when she, fresh from Nelson, had read Livy and Tacitus and Molière and Racine. Now they studied commerce, most of them, didn't they, and business management and marketing, and probably only two or three are left in French and Latin. Poor misfits—although, she heard, Bob Jones would sooner have them than new young property lawyers and cost accountants. But who else would? No one she can think of. Not Howie or any of his mates. Not Hopkins of Lupercal, who had liked the sound of it when she suggested that name for his company. 'Latin, eh? That'll do me,' and they drank to it. A grotto sacred to a Roman god? It had some class. He had not asked her which god.

So she did a nasty secret thing. And now Lupercal is in deep shit, as Howie would say, and in the papers daily, in the courts, and Hopkins and those men who had raised their glasses in her living room, with the city shining at their feet, are waiting judgment, waiting prison almost certainly, and her son Gordon, who had tried so hard to be big with them, is heading that way too and will not escape for all that he remains incurably small. Her clever little jab at them is punished in that way. It is rather Greek (she had done Greek too) and she has no energy to quarrel with it.

DAVID MITCHELL

David Mitchell (b.1940) has been performing his poetry since 1957, when he began his readings in Wellington cafés. His belief in poetry as spoken word is reflected in the structure of his poems on the page and has caused him to hold back from extensive publication; even so, his collection Pipe Dreams in Ponsonby *(1972) is recognised as being definitive of an era of revival and experimentation with new forms in New Zealand verse.*

the poetry reading

the girl at the window
is gazing out to sea

monsieur
has just

taken off
his camelhair coat

the maid is wasting time
at the mirror

monsieur
lights a cigar

madame engages
a friend

in conversation

footsteps on the
stair

like small alarms
precede the welcome

Sunbathers
1985

which must surely
follow

the new guests
taking off their

camelhair coats
wasting time

at the mirror
lighting cigars

engaging friends
in conversation

fabricating small alarms
for the pale girl

at the window
who is gazing

on the sea

Paris 1975

chess

these tall women
who

have just come
from mass

dressed in black
black
black

&

these pale men
who

have just come
from mass

dressed in black
black
black

do
not pause
to consider
the plaster
eyes
of
the virgin . . .

nor the bilious
eyes
of
the
beggar
in the square . . .

nor
the indolent
eyes
of the children
on the footpath . . .

nor
the crafty eyes
of the street artist
in his progress . . .

nor
the doleful eyes
of the poodle
on his lead . . .

they
are blind
these six
peasants

&

are led
slowly

to a white
white
white

taxi
      / one
        by
          one

by

one

very serious
very young

nun

Menton 1975

a woman amongst girls

she
goes

serenely

like a steady star
through

this firmament
as if it

had been
constructed

entirely
for her . . .

> i look at the works
> of matisse
> i look at the works
> of chagall
> i look at the works
> of renoir

& i am
reminded

that
it was . . .

& homage now
because of her

because of her grand
daughters

because of her grand
mothers

these banners of love
of delight

these banners
of praise

to the svelte
flesh

that scorns
serenely

> the perfection
> of the nights
> &
> the perfection
> of the days
> &
> what their passing
> might otherwise erase . . .

Menton 1975

MARILYN DUCKWORTH

Marilyn Duckworth (b.1935) is the author of nine novels including
Disorderly Conduct, *which won the New Zealand Book Award for*
Fiction in 1985; a volume of poetry; and a collection of short fiction,
Explosions on the Sun, *from which the following story is taken. She*
was awarded an OBE for services to literature in 1987.

All Those Daffodils

It's too much. First there were all those people picnicking on the roof, and now it's the lions.

Or could it be tigers? In any case, some large animal has been giving out its howling roar in the night. At first it sounded only on the edges of sleep so that I wondered if it was a dream. Then I dreamed about foghorns in the white Mediterranean. And when I woke up there were these wild animal roars coming from somewhere not too far away. The beach? Or the olive grove? Or close by in the hills above the boulevard? Has a tiger escaped from a circus? What will they do about it? Send out one of their police vans? Or a fire engine and crouching *pompiers* with a net?

The roaring stops. Then carries on, louder. It seems closer. If I open my bedroom window I might hear something huge crashing up in the bushes beyond the loquat tree. I wait, expecting at least to hear the sound of a siren. Authority going to investigate. But authority seems to be sleeping, like the rest of the town.

At last I grow tired of holding my head up to listen. The roaring becomes monotonous. It muffles as I begin to fall asleep.

I ask about the disturbance when I go to the *boulangerie* for my morning bread. The woman winds a baguette in a slip of paper. She looks at me as if I'm mad. She hasn't heard a sound.

In the olive grove an artist has set up his easel and is painting a view of the old town. He does this for postcards. Usually I steer clear of his space. But today I come up behind him and look to see if there are any wild animals in his sketch. A few pencil markings of the horizon and the bell-tower. No tigers burning bright.

They have mowed the grass for the musical performance and there is no wild clover for me to pick. In some places the grass is brittle and stubbly, like a harvested wheatfield. I see myself and my sister, Julie, gleaning in the fields behind our Surrey house—collecting fallen wheatears for our red hens. Later we sat in the itchy stubble and ate our baked potatoes stuffed with cheese, and our rice pudding, still slightly warm under the wrinkled skin. I had told Julie she would want to be a child again once she was grown up. But of course she hadn't believed me. I didn't believe it either. I'd read it in a book.

A motorbike roars by me as I walk down the Avenue Blasco Ibanez. Inside a workshop before the tunnel, an electric lathe whines. A train rumbles above the tunnel and I wait, pressed back against a dandelion weed, until it has passed. Wild noises everywhere. Are these the animals I heard in the night? I'd like to believe it, but that would be too easy.

Today is Bastille Day. I decide, on my evening walk, to pick something different from a clover or a blackberry. A dark stranger, I decide, with a vasectomy.

I prop on the sea wall, above the music and the dancers. Old women dancing together, and children. Young couples too. They aren't of my world. I catch myself smiling inanely at the old tunes, looking back at that world I had thought safely over the sea in England. Behind me, in the leaning inquisitive crowd, is a blond traveller, his bleached eyebrows illuminated by the light of the flame-eater who performs on the pavement. I walk away from the wall, watching the naked torso of the fire-eater. He gulps from a spirits bottle, throws his torch in the air, catches it. Flames roar from his mouth, silently. His torso is oiled and bronze.

That blond young traveller is behind me again. I walk fast to a point some yards along the wall, count to ten, turn around. He is there again. He smiles faintly. Lots of white teeth.

He is a Swede.

'I don't like Swedes,' I tell him, walking back to the cottage on his arm. 'Never liked swedes. We had them for school dinners. Nasty messy things. Ugh.'

'Nasty? I don't understand.'

His name is Leif. He pronounces it 'leaf'. I insist on 'life' instead, which is the Danish way. It sounds more positive.

'And I only fall in love with friends. I know it's prejudiced of me.'

'But I'm your friend,' he says, having known me three hours now, disguised in Indian cotton and semi-darkness.

'Friends are people who speak the same language,' I tell him.

'Ah—I understand you now. Language. Words, yes. That's very difficult.' He looks depressed.

If he doesn't like the scar on my leg it won't matter. I don't like his teeth. But the scar flares in my brain like the flame-eater's torch. If it weren't so deep—

'Look! Look!'

Fireworks arc in the sky, falling like blobs of jam into the dark sea.

'Is it much further?' he asks. 'We're nearly in Italy!'

'Yes—it's miles,' I say discouragingly. 'Up in the snake mountains. Two cobbled *sentiers*, fifty-four steps and *chiens méchants* barking in half a dozen gateways. Go on. You'd better go home. What's home in Swedish?'

He says it.

'Sounds Scottish. Are you mean too?'

'Excuse me?'

'Never mind.'

'As a matter of fact I'm coming with you,' he says. 'As a matter of fact I like you very much. I think I shall fall in love with you.'

'Do you have a vasectomy?'

'What?'

'Have you had the operation so you can't have children?'

'As a matter of fact—no.'

'Oh dear.' I stop on the wide pavement and begin to count on my fingers. Is it safe?

Now we stand on the grass verge in the centre of the broad Porte de France roadway, under the palm trees. I've taken off my shoes and the grass feels pliant, cushioned, as if it were backed with foam rubber. Leif picks a geranium and puts it between his teeth. He does a little stamping dance on the street and is nearly run down by a whining motor scooter.

I have put the geranium behind my ear and the spittle drools down my neck.

'Quick! We've got to get through the tunnel before the train comes!' I grab his hand and tug. His weight holds me back, like nightmare paralysis. Then he understands and runs, until it is he who is pulling *me* out of the tunnel. Just in time.

'Are you afraid of the trains?' he shouts as the twelve-thirty goods train crashes by. It sounds angry, vindictive.

'Only the wild ones.'

'I don't understand.'

'That's because you don't speak my language.'

'I am speaking very well. As a matter of fact I have a prize for English.'

'Oh—I've lost my flower.' I begin to laugh. 'Deflowered already and I've still got my knickers on.'

'What? You've no knickers on?'

'I still have them on. Oh dear. Words.' I lift up my skirt, turning my scarred thigh away from him, and display my cotton bikini pants.

'Forget the words. Yes.' He makes a grab for my left cotton buttock and misses.

'We've got fifty-four steps yet,' I tell him, dancing aside.

The iron gate lets us into the concrete wall. Up the curving, cool steps, past the gaping villa windows, to the second gate. I can't find the key. Leif fidgets. He needs a *pissoir*.

'Got it.' The gate opens and I lock it after us. Now we are locked in the aunt's garden together, this young man and I. Better than a blackberry. I shall stain my lips on him.

In the house he retreats to the bathroom. What will the aunt think of that? A Swedish cock in the Ladies' room. I am beginning to be nervous. His fingers will touch my scar. And the scar under my chin. Has he seen it? Oh, it's difficult to be ugly. Specially when it's relatively new. I never expected to be ugly. My sister would be pleased about that. You don't believe me? Ah, the rivalry of sisters can be as powerful as sexual jealousy. She died of a combination of these. And gave me my scars. But I have inherited the aunt's money—which was to be for her and Chris. Chris could still claim his share. If.

I'm really afraid now and plunge to turn out the main light which Leif has automatically turned on. I stumble in the dark and find a lamp switch. Now I can see him.

'You're so beautiful,' he says. And—'I love you.' He recites these words deliberately, like a child learning to read. 'The cat sat on the mat.' The meaning is not dissimilar. The cat leads him to her bed. Our hands reach out together to turn back the covers. Odd. As if we were a joined couple, practised in such gestures.

'The excuse for this is wine,' I explain. 'I'm so glad I'm drunk.'

'Are you? Oh no. I'm only sorry about the wine. I should like to be quite sober for you.'

'If you were, I wouldn't be here.'

'But this is your house.'

'I meant in this situation. You know the word situation?'

'Oh yes. Situation I come across often, in my business.'

'You're a businessman. Shit. I thought you were a student.'

'I'm thirty.'

'Ssh! I don't want to know.'

'Ah—Anna!'

'My name's Anne.' I spell it.

'Ah, Anna, I think we shall be very good with each other. I have a feeling I shall see much of you.'

'How long are you here for?'

'Three days.'

'Ah yes. Three days.' He has me in a curious position on the bed so that I cannot move. My body moves without me. I wrench myself free so that I can follow his feelings, undulating on the bed. The mattress, which is wider than the base, tips us onto the floor. We laugh and laugh, then—click—we are serious. This time—our third—we are making love.

'That was the same language.'

'Yes. I knew I should fall in love with you.'

'So this is love we've fallen into, is it?' I am laughing and laughing and my hair is all over my face, tickling. I wipe it aside.

'You have sense of humour.'

'Sense anyway.'

'Shall I come to see you again? Are your gates always locked?'

'Yes, always. I lock them against the trains, and the blackberries.'

'The black—ah you mean from Senégal? Afrique? Yes. But can I see you again?'

'Only at night. I'm busy in the day.'

He puzzles. 'Is there a bell at the gate?'

'Of course. But how shall I know if it's you?'

'Come down the stairs to the first bend. Call out and I'll whistle.'

'Yes—I like that. Whistle for me. Can you whistle like a train?'

'I can whistle your national anthem.'

'All right, that'll do. The aunt'll like that. It'll make her laugh.'

'The aunt? Your aunt? Where is she? The house down there?' This has startled him.

'No, no. Don't worry, she's only a ghost. Dead, you know. *Morte.*'

'Ah.' He is thinking of something or someone else. So am I. Chris.

Chris. He wells up inside me like the bulging sea, and breaks on hard rocks. Will I ever dare go back to that? Again. What in God's name am I doing on the floor with an albino Swede?

'Go home,' I say. Then I say it in Swedish as he has taught me. 'Go home now.'

The next day I regret it. Not Leif. I regret having refused to see him in the sunshine. After all, I'm not that ugly. And once the bitter aftertaste of red wine has left me, I feel an odd sensation. Loneliness. When have I ever minded solitude before? The banana leaf doesn't speak. There is no wind to animate it. Even the lizards have deserted me. I watch a passion-flower bud for some minutes to see if it will open. They always do this behind my back. Rude creatures. Sneaky. But there is only so much anger you can spend on a passion flower.

The workmen on the new apartment block call out to me as I pass.

'*Bonjour!* Have a good day!'

Cranes wheel in the sky, carrying the future in their jaws. I wonder where Leif is staying. How little curiosity I showed in him! As if he were indeed only a figment of my imagination and I could furnish the details later. It doesn't matter. He isn't Chris.

In the leafy square I buy an Orangina and squint at a nearby paper stand, stealing the headlines for myself. French newspapers bore me and I won't waste francs on them. 'Pimp arrested at Nice.' 'Twenty-one Rumanians flee into Austria.'

A young man has chalked a hard-luck story on the pavement, concerning his work permit. Now he sits, head on his knees, waiting for the public to drop coins in a square marked '*Merci*'. The square is modest, the coins have fallen wide. The young man makes no attempt to scoop them together. He is embarrassed, or asleep. The gendarmes read the message sternly, shrug and pass on. When he raises his head who will he be? Too dark for Leif. Too thin for Chris.

A trickle of flute notes rouses him. He lifts his face and watches a shabby, ageing satyr with rolled jeans and dark curls, who has placed his battered frying pan on the pavement opposite. The notes soar, white eyes roll in a dark, lascivious face. I look back at the young man without a work permit. Smooth, arrogant features. I seem to know him. And the music, rising, seems to help this knowledge. A few notes more and I shall remember. But the music stops. The ageing satyr shakes spittle from his flute.

The young man scoops up his coins at last, bending his head low. As he passes by my table he says some words I cannot catch. Even the language is unfamiliar. What does he want? Has he been spying on me?

Is he part of it? Part of what is happening here? Was his face one of those I saw in the secret cave? If cave is what it was. I'm sure it wasn't a dream. The first time I thought it was some sort of underground market or funfair. I love fairs—escaping onto ghost trains, into halls of mirrors. Dodgems. Julie and I liked the dodgems best. But I have returned to the spot—past the big Codec supermarket, the boats, the bodies sacrificing themselves on the sun's altar. I have returned home now at every hour of every day of the week. Nothing. No lights. Not even an opening in the wall.

Another evening I thought I saw it in the park—there were lights and music. But as I came closer the music faded. I thought it was the walls of the *raccourci*—the shortcut between apartment buildings—blurring the sound. But when I came out of the tunnelled steps, the lights had faded as well. Two lighted cigarettes moving above the dark shape of a dog. That was all.

Now I walk home. Twilight. Placing my feet carefully so as not to step in dog faeces. The mountains are in mist. I feel it falling through the darkness onto my skin. A warm moisture.

On the central grass verge. Leif is sitting between lemon trees. Jets of water have been turned on to drench the dry grass. He sits with his head on his knees, like the young man seeking the work permit. How do I know it is him? The white-blond hair, the red sweatshirt. If it isn't him I shall look pretty silly standing here beside him, my espadrilles darkening with water. He lifts his head and smiles.

'You're getting wet,' he says.

'Not as wet as you.'

'I like it. It's cool. I've been in the sun.' His shirt is sticking to his chest.

'You'll be cold soon.'

'Then I shall take it off. At your house.'

'Did you know I'd come past here?'

'Well you weren't at your house. I whistled and a big dog was very noisy, in the next garden.'

'I forgot the dog. I don't think he can get out.' And I laugh because I feel happy with my wet feet squishing in my shoes.

In my bed he says—'Last night I dreamed about you.'

'About me? What did you dream?'

'I dreamed I am making love to you, of course. And other things.'

'Then we don't need to make love now.'

'Oh yes we do. The real thing is more—more—better. And you? Have you dreamed of me?'

'I don't think so. Maybe. I can never remember who it was in my dream.' Suddenly I am struck with pleasure. 'Fancy you dreaming of me. *I* usually do the dreaming. That's nice of you to dream of me. And I expect I spoke Swedish in your dream?'

He thinks. 'Yes. Yes, that's right.'

'That's wonderful. I'm so pleased.' I sit up with joy. 'What are you doing?'

'I'm thinking.'

'Well don't think. Or lie down and think.'

In the morning I'm not afraid of Leif any more. He goes home today but that doesn't frighten me either. I feel good.

We eat outside the door, on the little balcony which is also a porch leading to the steps. Yoghurt and raisins for breakfast. The banana leaf nods recognition. A bush of long, fluted blooms, crinkled and cream-coloured, hangs near the table.

'Will you come back to Menton?' I ask.

'Yes. But when—?' He shrugs. 'It's a question of money. Will you be here?'

'When?' I remind him.

We shrug shoulders at each other. Sad, and not sad.

'What man did that to you?' he asks about my chin.

'Why should it be a man? Do you Scandinavians beat your women?'

'Not me.'

'It was a car crash. Last year. My sister crashed a car.' Well, it's nearly the truth.

'That's a bad thing to happen. But you are still beautiful. I still love you. And your sister? Is she beautiful?'

'Yes. Very beautiful. She's dead.'

'Oh, I'm sorry.'

'She'd rather be dead. Than this.' I stroke my scar.

'Oh no!' He looks at me, beginning to believe. 'Would she really? Oh no—she's wrong. Wrong. You see, you have found me!'

'See a pin, pick it up. All the day will bring you luck.'

'What is that?'

'A rhyme we used to say at school. Well, I've had a day's good luck. I'm happy.'

He seizes on this. 'I've made you happy? That's good. Will you walk with me to my hotel?'

Clouds like white phlegm mass at the back of the sky, hiding the edge of the sea. The boats are motionless inside the port, masts prickling. A strong, deliciously rotten smell rises on the breeze, something like Stilton cheese. An old, slow Frenchman walks his well-bred dogs in twin, red knitted coats. Their nostrils point delicately. The bitch is pregnant. The old man hawks and spits at our feet. Leif steps over it.

I go home alone. I am walking against a growing tide of tourists equipped with umbrellas, rolled Chinese mats, liloes, folding beach chairs. Their hopeful ugly legs and bellies make the daily pilgrimage. I walk away from the sea. The old bearded tramp, skin blackened with sun and grime, speaks to me briefly about salvation.

Later I hear Leif's train passing through Garavan station.

And now I'm alone again. I lean inside a hollowed olive tree and listen to a musical group playing in the park. I've been here so long I haven't had to buy a ticket. There were no ticket sellers at the gates when I came in before sundown. Of course I haven't been in this tree all that time, or I should be stiff. I've walked and sat, on seats and walls. Eaten my bread and salami, squirted a tomato on my skirt—not by design. Now I look down and find my sandalled feet swarming with ants. I take off the sandals, bang them together and walk barefooted up the path, away from the red and green spotlights. The olive trees are old. Nearly every one has a hidden hole for a love letter. There are no love letters, not to me, nor to anyone else that I can see. I am wondering how long it will last, this happiness. Three days is usual. Perhaps this time I can stretch it a little. There's a new smell in the hedges—not a death smell, a sensual, feathery smell. I haven't been able to discover yet what it is.

A young boy walking ahead of me stops short, turns in to the wall and wriggles his haunches. He is fishing inside his trousers. I hear the jet of his urine hissing in the dusty grass as I walk on past him. It is Tuesday evening and plastic rubbish bins are on the street. I walk briskly.

I always walked faster than Julie, even as a child. Walking home from school across the common, she'd dawdle infuriatingly. Once she sat down on the path and wouldn't move. She said her legs ached. I walked on, threatening not to come back. But of course I had to. She was so little. She looked so babyish sitting there in her little leather coat and pixie hat, blinking. I wanted to kick her. I wanted to pick her up like a doll and carry her home in my arms. I couldn't do either. I just had to wait until her legs got better and mine began to ache. I told her a few lies about school, to pass the time. I told her the boy she sat next to had had leprosy and they thought he was cured. But maybe not.

Funny to think *that* Julie is the Julie who sat beside me when the car crashed. What was she wearing? Not the hand-me-down leather coat and brown pixie hat.

Never mind. I shall have fishcakes with fennel and courgettes. Never mind what? I can't be losing my happiness already? I haven't thought of Chris for days. Or the future—that thing they wave at you like a flag when you're a child. As if it is somehow better than now. Nothing is better than now. (I run a few steps.) And won't be. Whoops—keep that future tense out of it.

Something odd happened last night. There was someone on the roof. At first I thought it was on the roof of the empty house below. I went out in my nightie and shone a torch. No one there. The roof, of course, is sloping and would be most uncomfortable to prowl about on. Why not trespass inside the house itself? Perhaps I was to have squatters for neighbours. The shutters on the house overlooking my steps have been wired shut, but the wire has long ago rusted. I shone the aunt's big torch in the window. All seemed quiet and undisturbed. I had a distinct impression this torch had shone in these exact corners on other occasions. It blinked out of sheer boredom, and went out. I shook the batteries about and it blinked on again briefly as I went back into the cottage.

The Lunch Table
1991

It was then I made the discovery that the footsteps were on my own roof. Footsteps, conversation, clinking noises. Whoever it was had climbed down the rounded tiles, toes curled for grip, and now they were picnicking on the flat part of the roof against the bank. I thought I heard wine glasses chink. 'Good health.' 'Bon appétit.' What would they be eating at two o'clock in the morning? It didn't matter. They were nothing to do with me. Let them get on with it. Perhaps they were friends of the aunt? Most of her friends—the ones I had met—were dull. Yawning English or simpering French. I looked at the ceiling hopefully. Sighed and went back to bed.

When I went down for my mail in the morning, armed with keys—two for the gates, one for the little metal box—I found several flat stones had been posted in the slot. And two leaves. I laid them out on the sunny wall and tried to read a message in them. They must mean something. At last I picked up the smoothest stone and took it upstairs with me. On the way I wondered if I'd discarded the best part of the message and was going away with the stone, the pips, as it were. But the core of an apple could be considered the best part. It depends if one wants to eat the fruit or grow something from it. I put my stone in the sun and waited to see what would develop.

I've gone deaf. This morning I couldn't hear the trains and so slept on and on, puzzled. I only wake as the trains tell me. Then gradually, through the silence, I began to hear my own deafness. It rang something like the inside out of a bell chime. Very strange. I walked down my steps. No footfalls. I began to lose belief in myself. Certainly the feeling of up—at the top of the steps—to down—at the bottom of the steps—was no different from walking along the street. If I lifted my wings I could fly.

I locked the gate behind me. Did I bang it? Who knows. And as I walked down the raccourci, I saw a train coming. It seemed to move very slowly, like drifting smoke, passing across my face. I felt responsible for making it move so slowly. After a long time it had gone. A dove flew across the back of my hand and there was a feather at my feet.

I sit now in a café, playing with the feather, stroking the back of my hand.

I've had this deafness before, since the accident. It always goes away. Now it goes. My aerial has been adjusted. A voice breaks in on me. A black voice. A black man is holding a white shawl at me, calling the cheapness of his wares. I stare at him, startled by the crash of sound. He backs away as if he thinks I am about to stab him with the feather. He has recognised me in any case, and knows I'm not a holiday-maker to be tempted by his shawls and beads. Ah, sound. All the noises locked up in my head rush out again to externalise themselves. There is room in my mind for thought.

I think about Chris, and when I came away. Give it time, he said. He didn't mean the scars on my body—these have healed up as well as they ever will. He meant the thing between him and me. It's interesting that expression—'between us'. 'What exactly is there between you?' my sister Julie had asked me. Of course the point was that there was *nothing* between us any more. All distance, all impediments had been dissolved so that we were touching and one. It was precisely this, this closeness that had terrified her so. But now. She would be glad to know that there is something between us now. Land and sea. And her own death. Give it time, he said.

He was carrying a yellow chrysanthemum to put on his wife's grave.

He didn't want to come—'Julie wouldn't like it.' He was the guilty one. My scars had absolved me from guilt.

'I wanted to die at first,' he told me. 'I had plenty of tranquillisers to do it. My friends gave them to me, being kind.'

'Why didn't you?'

'Because of the daffodils. All those daffodils. They came with the tranquillisers. It was blackmail. They blackmailed me into staying alive—with daffodils.'

'The sun's going,' I reminded him. 'You'd better go quickly or they'll close the cemetery.'

I remember the daffodils. They had given me daffodils too, in hospital. I understand the stalks are lethal. I could have munched my way across the Lethe. But I didn't want to die.

Julie wanted to die. Well, one of us had to do it—Chris is not divisible by two. It made sense at the time—the accident. It does make sense—yes. Why then do I seem to have damaged some connecting thread in myself? As if Chris and I had depended on Julie to hold us together. Little Julie—how could she have that strength?

Does Chris know or care that it was me sitting in the driver's seat, not Julie, when the car hit the old elm tree? Of course, it could have gone wrong—it could have been me that went to the crematorium in a shiny box. We took that risk, Julie and I. I'm glad it wasn't me. I didn't want to die. But living isn't so easy.

So I've run away to the aunt's cottage.

But I keep feeling someone is watching.

I am sitting in my doorway in the sun, leaning back on my elbows and letting the sun pour its warmth all over my face. My elbows are slippery with perspiration and begin to slide on the tiles. Salt sweat drops ooze and trickle out of my hair and into my eyes. How funny, I think. I'm crying backwards.

Did I cry at the time? They say it's healthier to cry a lot of tears. Do they advise the bereaved to drink lots of fluid, like nursing mothers? I'm sure they should. But I've never been very concerned with fitness. Now they say jogging causes heart attacks. Next they will say tears are the worst thing for grief. I can handle grief. No one goes mad from grief. What was that argument I had with the therapist before I came away?

In any case, here I am, brown, relaxed and crying backwards in the sunshine. Nothing mad about me.

My sister and I used to love the sun as children. We would take all our clothes off and run away down the road onto the common. It drove our mother frantic. She saw dirty old men under every hawthorn bush.

'Julie! Anne!' she used to call, running the names together as if they were one. 'Julianne!'

One evening when she had put us to bed while the sun was still up, we made our protest. We hitched up our nighties, giggling, and sat our bare bottoms out the window. The last rays of the sun touched us.

The salt sweat is getting in my eyes. It stings. How can it hurt so much?

Enough sun for today. When I stand up my head reels with it.

WITI IHIMAERA

Witi Ihimaera (b.1944) is the author of four novels, including Tangi *and* The Matriarch, *and three collections of short stories. After resigning from the diplomatic corps and a posting to New York, he returned to New Zealand in 1990. His most recent work has been the play* Two Taniwha, Toa *(a musical) and* The Clio Legacy *(with Dorothy Buchanan). He is editor of the six-volume series on Maori writing,* Te Ao Marama. *The following extract is from a novel he has been completing while in France, entitled* Nights in the Garden of Spain.*

A Walk Along the Crocodile's Tail

Seagulls wheel and skirl across the Crocodile's Tail. Rebecca has climbed the whole length from the jaws, snapped open on the beach, to the tail lashing out in the deep water. It is high tide and part of the Crocodile, where the body and tail are joined, is submerged. Poor little Miranda is trying to gauge when to wade across. Every time she starts to venture across another wave comes crashing through the gap.

'Becka,' Miranda wails. 'Becka.' Even her wand, the long stick with the star tacked on that her sister has made for her, is ineffectual against the might of Neptune.

Annabelle and I are on the beach watching from afar. I go to help but Annabelle restrains me.

'No,' she says. 'They'll work it out.'

Indeed Rebecca, sighing that 'Why did I have such a hopeless little sister?' sigh, climbs down. Her instructions to Miranda drift over the waves to us. 'When I count three, darling, jump onto that rock and then that rock. Okay?'

'Come and carry me over,' Miranda sobs.

'You can do it,' Rebecca answers.

'I truly can't, Becka.'

Rebecca surprises us with her sharpness. 'Miranda, you are such a wimp,' she answers again. 'Now one, two, THREE.'

Before she can even think about it, Miranda is splashing across the gap. Whoosh comes a wave but too late, too late, ha ha ha! Miranda is across, taking Rebecca's hand and being led to the top of the tail.

'I'm the King of the castle and you're the dirty rascal!'

Her piping voice ends in a little wheeze and cough. Quickly she reaches for her inhaler and

The Pink Villa
1990

takes a puff. Looks at us, hoping we haven't seen.

I settle back on the sand. The picnic food looks as if it has been machinegunned by Miranda's mouth. The blanket is littered with half-eaten buns, pizza and half-consumed bottles of soda.

'That younger child of yours,' Annabelle says, good-humouredly excluding herself from the parental process. 'She's such a terror with food. Picking one thing up and putting it down. Picking up another. And she won't go anywhere without that silly wand.'

'We shouldn't stay out too long,' I say. 'I think she's coming down with something.'

'Oh it's just psychosomatic,' Annabelle answers. 'She was coughing a little just before we left the house. Anyway, we have to fend for ourselves now.'

Annabelle starts to clear up. As she bends and reaches I notice how much slimmer she has become.

'So how much have you lost?' I ask.

'Can you tell?' she answers, pleased. 'About a stone.'

'It looks good,' I continue. 'Obviously going to the gym and whatever else you're doing is paying dividends.'

'I'm getting on with my life,' she answers, nodding to herself. 'Yes.' Finishes packing up. 'Let's go for a walk.'

'What about the girls?'

'They'll be okay. Come on. I'll race you to the point.'

With that she is off, sprinting down the beach, her toes digging into the sand. I sprint after her, and people on the beach yell encouragement. 'Go, go, GO.'

She is like Diana, the Roman Goddess of the Hunt. And like Diana she has golden apples, one of which she tosses, just as I am coming abreast of her.

'The girls!'

Her eyes register alarm. She points to the Crocodile's Tail.

I falter. Look behind. The girls are waving and shouting in the sun. Feel something shove me in the small of my back. Trip and fall. And the trickster Annabelle sails gaily on, silvering the air with her laughter.

Now we are returning from the point. Annabelle has threaded an arm through mine. It is just like old times. If anyone was looking they would not know the turmoil that lies beneath this happy picture. They would see, simply, a man, a woman and two lovely children.

'So, what did you want to talk to me about?' Annabelle has been chatting happily but now stops. Colours. 'Come on,' I nudge. 'Don't be coy.'

She looks at me, sideways, through her eyes. Watching me carefully. The Crocodile's Tail has always been the place where we have been able to confess the small intimacies of our lives.

'I've been asked out on a date.'

I laugh out loud and she is offended.

'Don't you think I'm attractive enough for men?' she asks.

'No, it's not that,' I answer.

'Then what!' She moves away from me and stops on the beach, arms akimbo.

'God,' I sigh, 'you take the cake. I'm happy for you, that's all. You take my breath away.'

She stays apart, still uncertain. Then takes my arm again.

'It's just a date after all,' she shrugs. 'Nothing serious. But it's a validation. I've been really bruised, you know. When a man leaves a woman for another woman that's bad enough. But when it's for another man—'

We walk on a while in silence.

'Is he anyone I know?' I ask.

'Actually, yes,' she confesses. 'Do you remember George?'

'The Greek?' I answer. An old boyfriend of Annabelle's. The Hellespont ram. Oh no.

'He's been divorced for a while. We bumped into one another a few weeks ago. He's been pestering me ever since.'

'I'll bet,' I say, and Annabelle catches my cynicism.

'Look,' she answers, 'the world is full of solo mothers. It's really hard out there. I have to take my chances. I'm not looking for anything more than a nice man to take me out to a nice dinner at some warm restaurant, and nothing more. Okay?'

I nod and pull her close to stop her from being hurt. She pokes me with a finger.

'Oh, YOU,' she says. Then, 'My therapist has told me I must start looking forward. Sometimes the only way I've been able to manage that is to pretend to myself that you have died. Not left me, but died.'

'Gee, thanks.'

'I know that might sound harsh but thinking of you as dead makes it much easier to stop hoping that you'll come back.'

I stop and stare at her. She looks back at me. I can see Rebecca staring at me from out of those eyes. Tears spilling.

'Damn you, Derek. You were supposed to look after me. But you didn't. You forgot to hold me tight. You let a gap happen, a space for the wind to come between us.' Then, 'And by the way, Miranda says you come around to the house sometimes. She's seen you sitting out there in the car watching the house. Late at nights. It's got to stop.'

'I just come by to make sure—'

'We can look after ourselves, Derek.'

The afternoon is turning cold. The clouds are hurtling across the sky. The waves are white-tipped and the crocodile is trying to dislodge my two princesses into the sea. There to snap them both in half with its jaws.

'Girls?' Annabelle calls. 'Time to go home.'

'Okay, Mummeee—'

Rebecca clambers down and, when they get to the gap in the tail, piggybacks Miranda across. Miranda is coughing as she runs up to us.

Rebecca's eyes are shining with joy and happiness. Although the light flickers when I drop her, Miranda and Annabelle at their house, it returns again with all the energy she can muster.

'It was good to be a family again, wasn't it Dad?'

'Yes, darling. Yes.'

The Connoisseurs
1985

LISA GREENWOOD

Lisa Greenwood (b.1955) began writing in 1983 and published her first novel, The Roundness of Eggs, *in 1986. Her second novel,* Daylight Burning, *was published in 1990. She is at present completing a medieval novel begun in France and originally set there, but relocated to the fen landscape of East Anglia, partly because of her attraction to that part of England, but principally because of the greater accessibility of research materials.*

Moonflowers

Dear xxx

One day I'll explain my silences, the dearth of sunny postcards dropping in your letterbox. But for now I want to say I'm in the room, my feet are cool on the tiles, I have your gift, I'm contemplating a change of career. It's true! The welter of sensations and impressions of France resists translation into words. My novel waits, pregnant yet refusing any schedule but its own. I've taken to writing fragments. Pieces. I'm optimistic however and today, in the absence of creative ferment, I'm brewing soup—at least I've rehydrated something bright as duck weed from a sachet and it steams pleasantly on the little burner, exuding aromas of onion and herbes de Provence.

In Codec this morning, after selecting my sachets and rattling bottles of vin ordinaire, I purchased a small cake, purely for the pleasure of naming it aloud.

'Une religieuse, s'il vous plaît,' I said, confidently, overly loudly perhaps.

In some respects that's my problem. I sense a presence in this place so powerfully, so tangibly, I want to state its name, to give it voice, to write it out and yet . . . I can't for the life of me tell what it's called.

The cake I purchased was a nun, a choux pastry with large puff to represent the body and diminutive puff atop, the whole welded with cream and dressed in a habit of pure decadence. Chocolate, that is. I carried it back to the room in a box and separated the portions, placing the head at one end of the table, the torso at the other. Then I found myself circumnavigating that item of furniture, clockwise if I recall, muttering incantations in neither French nor English but a hybrid I'm working on. Sprinkling a little Perrier. it was a ritual, undoubtedly, a primal rite.

I've been attending Mass, I ought to say, but fail to understand the words. At ten on Sunday mornings the bells toll and I put on my blue dress, the one with mother of pearl buttons and a tiny tear in the hem where I snagged it on a moped in the street. The Cathedral St Michael—

more Italian than French as you know with its barrel vaulting and baroque excesses—is always well attended. Beggars ply their trade at the doors and I pass eyes lowered, shamefaced.

You mentioned the monastery above Menton. L'Annonciade. Recently I've taken to loitering in the crypt (I justify my actions as research). One of the monks—a real monk in cowl and tonsure—or it may be he's balding in compliance with the tradition of his order—has a reasonable grasp of English but varies in his willingness to oblige. On fruitful days he's identified relics for me quite cheerfully. Ball joints, fingers, thigh bones and shreds of parchment he assures me are flesh. None of these pieces are easily recognised. From the martyrs, he nods. What martyrs? I need to know. I'm desperate for detail. He shrugs, drawing me inevitably back to his favourite exhibit, a piece of grizzled tin and cloth. It is, he explains, fuselage from a Zeppelin shot down in the war. A fragment of an airship, mysteriously elevated to the status of holy remains. It always makes me laugh. I love emerging from the chapel into light, the particular light of the Côte d'Azur. I love the cypress trees, the terrace of swept earth, the panorama of ocean and mountains—the roofs of Menton perched audaciously between.

Every time I leave L'Annonciade I purchase a card depicting St Francis as a soul of simple intellect. I have a number of these in the room. I often scrutinise his face. Is it the asymmetry I'm drawn to or jug ears? The halo or stigmata or strange shade of blue? Between looking at the cards I sometimes gaze at the print by the door. A certain similarity comes to exist. The blessed Virgin compared to a jug of pure water and infant Jesus to a lamp. The patron saint of ecology compared to a painting by Colin McCahon. Alongside the print I've attached postcards of the lemon festival, life-sized windmills, locomotives and a model of Le Moulin Rouge made entirely of citrus fruit.

I've been thinking of treasures brought back to the room. My pièce de résistance is a snake skin I found high in the mountains, sloughed onto the edge of a scrubby sage bush. It's thinner than tissue and only faintly pigmented but quite generously sized. Our mutual friend identified its source as a grass snake—non-venomous—then informed me the small snakes I've been observing in the river at Sospel aren't snakes at all but slow worms. I've taken solace in the understanding a slow worm is at least a legless lizard not a worm.

Another talisman I have on the deep window ledge is a bead. The Duchess—you must know the one (there can't be that many duchesses in the South of France—or can there?) came to the room seeking information on KM. Early in our conversation however it became clear, to me at least, she'd researched the subject as thoroughly as I. The curious thing was as we spoke her beads broke and went jumping, pinging in a frenzy on the floor. For me it terminated a certain tension—for her, I felt, created one. We gathered the stones at the time but later I found just the one.

Anyway, an outcome of her visit was my visit to the Princess Grace Irish Library in Monaco. The prospect of an English language library thrilled me (you know I'm sorely troubled by the shortage of books). I went on a Tuesday. The train was full and I thought I imagined a hand on my thigh the first time. But when we entered a tunnel there was no mistaking the intentions of a fellow passenger. At times I despise having no French—or so little it barely counts. Abuse doled out in English is ineffectual here. The man, a languid Latin, smiled.

In Monaco I ran up the steps to the palace and entered the maze of the old town. When I located the address I couldn't get through the door and raised a minor fracas in the street. The gentleman who finally let me in was discreet and immaculately well mannered whilst managing to convey his displeasure at my unannounced arrival. I understood they were of course very busy preparing for the impending celebration of James Joyce. A multiplicity of events was planned and scholars would be attending from many countries. Guinness would be freighted in, green garments donned, and Irish nannies (real ones) provided for those inconvenienced by children. So distracted was I by the sheer quantity of books I scarcely followed these details. The Princess Grace Library is a bibliotheca. A museum. The misunderstanding lay I suppose in my assumption that a library is a place one borrow books, or reads them anyway. A second man who very kindly showed me around, did so by sliding book after book—signed first editions and so on—from the shelves, consulting a slip on the inside cover and stating the volume's value in pounds. Many pounds. Halfway through the tour I blurted my request—would it be possible for me to come in sometimes and read (the mundane books would do, reference material, encyclopaedias!)? My host looked distressed and took small shuffling steps then extended one hand, requesting my business card. I've never had a business card. He would, he said, have to consult. And so it was (hovering in the hall between the room housing the Mungo Park private collection and the Beckett display) that my pregnant novel—which had in days preceding my visit become an Irish novel—switched back to something indeterminately European.

On my way home I popped into the Anglican Church Library and found to my very great pleasure a Bruce Chatwin that I hadn't read before.

'He was here in the South of France,' the elderly woman told me, 'but already dying then and in a wheelchair.'

On the Promenade de la Mer the tiny climbing roses are in bloom. And moonflowers—not only the white ones familiar from New Zealand, but lemon, peach and apricot. The Mémorial Kathérine Mansfield is tranquil (particularly now work has halted on the new apartment block).

I think of you here more than you'd have any way of knowing. sometimes I wander to the station and sit a while, gazing back at the limestone cliffs, the burgeoning gardens of Garavan, the pink villa, the curve of railway lines. When unable to absorb a fraction more I wander back. Now it's getting warmer lizards can be seen on the external walls of the room. Sometimes they traverse the windows and I'm able to examine their fishy bellies and elongated toes—each terminating in a sucker—through the glass. Not a day passes I'm not surprised by something—astonished in fact.

With much love

LLOYD JONES

Lloyd Jones (b.1955) has published two novels, a collection of short fiction Swimming to Australia, *from which 'Me, Clark and Wilder' is taken, and a highly acclaimed book about his travels in Albania,* Biografi, *published also in Great Britain and the United States.*

Me, Clark and Wilder

La Turbie is an old Roman town in the French Maritime Alps. Beside the tree-lined cafés the tour buses disgorge their passengers, and it is here the rock climbers turn off and drive to a promontory which overlooks the tiled rooftops of Monte Carlo. Cars with licence plates with Italy, the UK, Germany, huddle here.

Abutting the carpark are the wonderful limestone cliffs with names such as 'Mort au con'. There are easier climbs and with more pleasant names. 'Chausson aux pommes', for example.

Clark Griffen, the Canadian writer, turned up in sandshoes. The pastels of good clothes and shoes worn by climbers camouflage their practical aspect. Climbing shoes combine the virtues of a running shoe and a ballet shoe. The shoe is light but with a hard narrow toe able to probe a crevice or lesion.

It was a gorgeous afternoon. The spring rains had just finished, and the air was left thin, and the chalk had been washed from the rocks. I think we climbed Les Fleurs, a small easy outcrop.

The track takes you past the abandoned military quarters, and runs along the foot of the first lot of rockfaces. Far below was the toyland of Monte Carlo. But we were up here, in the lap of the gods, the sunshine, the warm rock; and the blue sea without hint of pollution spread south, east and west. The grunts of climbers could be heard, and the tinny jangle of the carabiners. Otherwise there was a concentrated quiet, except for Clark, who kept taking stock of our whereabouts. All the way to Les Fleurs, every so often Clark pulled on my arm—'Look at this! Will you look at where we are.' He said this with the intimation of some slight wrongdoing: of our having got away with something.

Clark was also excited at finding another writer—although it had been Liz Griffen who, one morning one week ago, boldly knocked on the door of the Isola Bella. She was enrolled in a literature course at the Canadian University in Villefranche. Mansfield was on the list, which is what had brought her to Isola Bella.

Liz Griffen gazed at the bronze bust of Mansfield on the wall. With some deference she touched the old green bedspread with its moulting corrugation. The prints of old New Zealand failed to engage her and before long, regrettably, she brought her eye to bear on the bookcase with its worn detective and mystery stories that my predecessors had failed to return to the

English Church Library in Menton.

Clark duly appeared in the doorway. He measured the walls with his ungainly arm span. He gazed at the ceiling and scuffed the tiled floor, poked his head through the curtains. 'Bathroom out the back? Fantastic. This is fantastic.' Hands in pockets, he spied the writing material on the desk. 'Hey, teletype. You use teletype too.' He walked over to the desk and craned to read the page in the typewriter.

'Wilder, eh?' he said.

'Clark,' his wife gently admonished.

'Oh I'm sorry. There I go. Hey, listen . . . Oh God, isn't this what I always do?' He held his head in his hands.

The thing is, he told me, he was a writer too. Oh nothing much. Nothing like this. Nothing profound.

He said he wrote 'commercial stuff'.

'Clark, there's nothing wrong with what you write,' said his wife.

'I know, I know. I always feel this stupid need to apologise . . .'

'There's nothing wrong with what you do,' said his wife.

'Hey, look, we barge in here. We're holding up the poor guy from work,' Clark said. 'What about Teddy and Mouse?'

'Did you lock the doors, Clark?'

They had their kids waiting in the car—the same age as my children it turned out, so I invited them down to our house. The building site opposite our house was in full cry; Friday is concreting day, and we had to stand out the back of the house under the lemon trees to be heard.

It seems Clark had always wanted to be a writer. Other circumstances demanded he become a lawyer. He was unhappily successful. Then one day he decided, enough.

Coincidentally, or deliberately, he never did say, he had looked up a list of birthdays for the famous and infamous, and happened to notice the centenary of Jack the Ripper approaching. In a fit of vision and giddiness he gave up his practice, bought a typewriter, learnt to type, rented a house for the writing, and inside three months had *Death Merchant* written. Then what? He was still on this high. The America's Cup was being contested in Fremantle. He got a friend to mock up a jacket, and on the strength of this dummy the book was sold to a small Chicago publishing company. Clark·spent two weeks in Fremantle. Loved Australia. Raced back to Toronto and wrote *America's Cup* inside six weeks. It was duly listed in the *New York Times* book review section as one of the season's best books. But it was *Death Merchant* that had turned things around. Good reviews in Canada alerted the agents in New York. Clark chose the biggest. Next thing he was fifty thousand dollars richer, and *Death Merchant* was being 'sprayed' into supermarkets across America.

At La Turbie while I pulled on my shoes I started to explain a few things, mostly cautionary aspects, about rock climbing.

'Treat the rock like you would a narrative,' I said.

A foot placed here will have consequences further up the rockface. The idea is to trace a vague line. Don't hurry your moves but, equally, hesitation can lead to a gluey situation. Next thing your knees are shaking: the way up appears impossible, and the way down has mysteriously vanished.

'Above all,' I said, 'concentrate.'

Les Fleurs is nothing more than a warm-up exercise. The only way to fall would be to throw yourself from the face. But all too soon Clark had forgotten my cautions, and was talking about 'writing' again.

He was saying that before the success of *Death Merchant* he and Liz used to fly down to Manhattan for a weekend of hobnobbing with the rich and famous. By Saturday afternoon they were ensconced inside the Russian Tea Room.

'The first time I ever walked in there, I felt like a stiff. You know,' he said, 'like walking onstage to receive a leaving certificate. Now? Now it's no big deal.'

They had been in the Russian Tea Room while Woody Allen was there eating cheesecake. Norman Mailer was another regular. Warhol. Another time their table was smack up against the table of Truman Capote who was entertaining a party of people. Crying their eyes out. And after a while Clark and Liz laughed too. You couldn't help yourself. Laughing with Capote that time in the Russian Tea Room.

You can virtually walk up Les Fleurs. But there is one interesting overhead hold which calls for some technique, and with the concentration it required I had tuned Clark out.

The next I heard was a rather meek request from below. I had instructed him to follow and copy my holds, but he was several metres off the line of the climb.

'Looks like I need some help here, eh.' He managed to sound calm. Understated. His chin, usually varnished with some kind of after-shave treatment, dripped sweat. As I say, his voice was composed, quite a stranger to the alarm gripping his face.

I had to drop maybe three metres, come over one, and climb up to Clark's stranded position. There is nothing heroic in what happened next. If anything I am guilty of negligence. Clark appeared secure. So I didn't hurry beyond a normal descent.

I was directly underneath Clark's foothold, such as it was, when he decided he could hold on no longer. He simply let go, and without surprise or complaint had begun to freefall down the rockface. I had a very good foothold, and smacked him against the face until he found a foothold. It happened very quickly, in a matter of seconds.

At the bottom of Les Fleurs he walked around in a small circle. He slapped his sides and took deep breaths. I think he was mostly relieved. 'Look at me,' he said. 'Look at my arms. My legs. I'm shaking. I might never stop. I could have died. I can't believe this. I should be dead. Hey,' he said, resting his hand on my forearm. 'Hey, you know what I'm going to do . . . No listen. No bullshit.' He was still shaking, but focused and earnest with it. 'I want you to meet Al. You have got to meet Al.'

Al was Clark's agent, a kind of literary oracle for Clark. Al says this, Al says that. Clark said, 'Al says all novels can be boiled down to a three-act play.' Or, 'Those bookshops playing Bach are bullshit. Carpet and a coffee machine and they think they can charge a higher margin. Books should be in supermarkets. Warehouses. Why should a book be any different from Heinz baked beans.'

'You have got to meet Al,' Clark said. 'Listen, I'm going over there in three weeks. I need more money. You write a synopsis of what you're writing and I'll see Al gets it. I owe you this buddy.'

It was useless protesting. I don't mind gratitude, but it was nothing, really. He had fallen maybe two feet. But Clark felt he had a debt to repay.

He shook his head. And breathed mightily. Glad to be alive.

'You have got to meet Al. Those small print runs. Hey.' He ticked his fingers as if at a bad habit.

We had a beer in a café at La Turbie. Clark asked what I happened to be writing. 'See, I need to know, so I can present it the best way to Al.'

I told him I was writing about goats. Yes. It's surprising how bits of disconnected story choose the oddest moments to come together. I described to Clark a journey undertaken by a New South Wales doctor late last century to purchase a herd of high quality wool-bearing goats from a place in the Urals. A town meeting had been called and the doctor, no doubt with adventure in his heart, had volunteered to undertake the journey. He set out on foot from the Urals with two thousand goats and walked across what was then known as Asia Minor. In Calcutta he lost five hundred goats to disease. Elsewhere he had had to fight off hill bandits. Customs. Bureaucracy. And now he had to find a ship to take him and the goats back to Australia. It was an epic tale.

'And a true one,' I emphasised.

But Clark's disappointment was plain to see.

'You have to understand,' I said. 'It isn't really about goats but a travel story. Retracing the doctor's journey in the latter part of the twentieth century.'

'Goats, eh,' he said. 'If I introduce you to Al you have to promise me you won't mention goats. Please, you have to promise me this. No goats.'

'Well, nothing is set in print, yet. It's just an idea,' I said.

Still, the damage was done. I could see Clark was still thinking 'goats', and given to second thoughts. Goats gave way to professional pride, and I told him about Wilder, the prison artist and escaper.

Clark's eyes lit up.

'A prison escaper. Now you're talking!'

Clark's wife rang the next day. She said Clark had woken from a deep sleep about 4 a.m. Liz said, 'He sat up in bed, shouting, "I coulda been killed!"'

Then Clark came on the phone—'How's that synopsis coming along?'

At La Turbie I had told Clark a few facts about Wilder. He was a car thief, a prison escaper and, later, a prison artist. And, briefly, a folk hero in the sixties. Clark, of course, saw a man hurtling up creekbeds ahead of tracker dogs with thick necks straining at leashes. He saw Wilder 'sprayed' out across America. Money. A film contract. Maybe a mini-series option.

'Listen,' he said. 'We can meet in Monte Carlo. We can discuss how to deal with Al there.'

Clark met me off the train. Hands in the pockets of his corduroy jacket, he stood on the platform tall and dignified above the swelling mob of backpackers. He wore the same white shoes that had failed to hold him on the rocks at La Turbie.

We walked up the hill to the old town and found a café opposite the lines of tourists entering the Jacques Cousteau aquarium. I ordered a *chocolat chaud*, and Clark, a small black Nescafé.

He talked about the first time he went to Al's office. An old brownstone in Greenwich Village. You walked up the stairs, and in a glass box was the first draft of Al's protégé Brad Seager's *After Dark*. All kinds of Seager memorabilia lined the staircase and reception area. Inside Al's office Clark sank up to his waist in a deep brown leather couch, and just listened to the man talk. Al might sell commercial, but he knew art. He had taught renaissance literature at Yale. But hey, now he was out in the real world. He confessed to Clark he was a little worried about Seager's form. Success had made him soft and unmotivated. In Clark's

Death Merchant he sensed something of the young Seager. A good sense of pace. Sharp scene evocation. A bright slap of blood and violence, but by no means sodden with it.

Clark had got to meet Seager. Great guy. At Al's suggestion Seager loaned Clark some old drafts to study.

'The thing about Al, he thinks conceptually,' Clark was saying. 'You got to have this Wilder guy mapped out, so Al can slot him into the marketplace. Five . . . maybe ten minutes is all you're going to get with him. In that time you have to sell Wilder. That's all you get. Start off on the wrong note and his eyes will glaze over before your second heartbeat.'

'I don't know, Clark,' I said.

'Hey. Come on. It's not the usual bullshit about money tainting the goods?'

'No,' I said, and it wasn't.

'Listen,' he said, and reached over to clasp my forearm. He spoke very seriously, like someone who has successfully returned from a reconnaissance mission across enemy lines with crucial information.

'That first time I was in Al's office there was a pile of covering letters on his desk. Al showed me. This high,' he said, and he released my arm to paddle his hand six inches above the table. 'So, anyway, Al was called out of the office and I sneaked a look. These were quality people. Names from literary magazines and reviews. And their covering letters. Shameless. Talented, talented people, begging Al to take them aboard and save them.'

Clark settled back with his Nescafé. After a while he said, 'Hey, will you look where we are. Will you look at this!'

Monte Carlo was Clark's territory. His characters frequented casinos; were comfortable in evening dress; ran drug-boats into port from Algiers. He had until December to organise this case into a manuscript. Al said he was 'allowed' four characters. At least one had to be a woman, but concessions could be made there. Two of the characters had to be American, and that was more or less mandatory. The storyline was some drug odyssey. Al had contacts all over the globe. Arrangements had been made for Clark to cross the Mekong into the Burmese sphere of the Golden Triangle. He had ridden horseback in the company of Thai police. In Paris, he had been taken to a vast subterranean area beneath the Charles de Gaulle airport, where dozens of North Africans caught smuggling drugs were detailed. He met pregnant women who, it turned out, were not pregnant. He was shown LSD film cooked into clothing. In Clark's book the North Africans were the bad guys.

I saw North Africans every day on the building site across the railway line from the Isola Bella. The site was run by a short grumpy-mouthed Italian. his wife looked to be from the south, as well. On Fridays she came by with the payslips for the North African workmen, who lined rue Webb Ellis which departs avenue Kathérine Mansfield for the Gare du Garavan. The foreman's wife would approach heavily in her flat black shoes. Her dress code was one of mourning. The payslips were in her back handbag and, as she moved down the line, in the face of each workman arose the dreadful possibility that his pay had been overlooked, or that today a mistake of some kind had been made. The foreman folded his hands behind his back while his wife dealt with complaints. The North Africans still to receive their pay grew increasingly anxious. Their arms fell quite lifeless at their sides.

Until Clark mentioned it, I hadn't thought of them as drug-runners.

'Any industry has its rank and file,' he pointed out. Then he said, 'So what about this Wilder guy?'

Artist's Family on the Terrace
1990

I was writing about Wilder, but mostly I was writing about failed immigrants. How, in a small country, no one let go of old friends. The community was too small to permit lives to be shed. No redundancies here mate. In the event of an attempted escape old photographs were mockingly presented. Old IDs. The old life. Paroled after a decade spent in prison, Wilder attempts to launch himself on an artistic career. Within six months the old crims have looked him up. 'This isn't you, George,' they must have said; not in so many words of course. Wilder didn't see the year out before he was back in court, listening to his counsel describe him as a 'weak, impressionable man'.

One afternoon, a week before Clark was due to fly out to New York, he dropped by the Isola Bella to ask if I had a photograph of Wilder.

'Al might need something more to go on,' he said. 'Every bit helps.'

I did have a photograph of a self-portrait. Strictly speaking it isn't a self-portrait (prison artists were not allowed mirrors) but the painting is by Wilder of a 1970 news photograph of himself in handcuffs being led from the Rotorua Police Station to a waiting paddy wagon.

No embellishment of the news photograph has interested Wilder, unless a case is to be made for the eyes where he has settled for dashed off lines, the sort of brushstroke meant to signify seagulls in the high right hand corner of seascapes in cheap seafood restaurants. Elsewhere there is a fullness to his cheeks, and the pug nose as ever, tumescent as a piece of ripened fruit about to scatter its seed. The rest is simple reportage: an electrician's peaked cap, a v-neck sweater, a windcheater. The dark bristly start to a beard. But always it is the eyes that delay me, and I think they were the reason I didn't show the photo to Clark. Out of loyalty. Yes, loyalty. Look at the eyes and you ask yourself, are Wilder's eyes still undilated slashes seeking obscurity? Does he remain haunted by the prospect of the telephone ringing, the unexpected knock on his door, and the unimaginable: his life 'sprayed' out to supermarkets across America?

'Well,' Clark said with disappointment. 'A photograph always helps. It may spark off a cover idea, and with Al that can be enough. You know.'

'Gee, Clark, I'm sorry.'

'Well,' he said. 'I've come all this way. We might as well have a drink.'

We passed Clark's drug-runners on the building site, and wandered towards the old town in search of a café. Old photographs show a narrow beach running the length of Garavan to the old town of Menton. The newer postcards with tanned melon breasts fail to reveal the new marina and its retaining wall of large round boulders. In between, and at the base of these boulders, has formed a detritus of old rubbish, beer and wine bottles, and various plastics. A gentle swell pushes in there, gurgles and slurps out to the depths. In May the German tourists settle over these rocks. At night itinerants unravelled their soiled bedrolls over these same rocks still warm from the afternoon sun.

One week later I might have pointed out Wilder to Clark. I might have said, 'Look, over there.' Among the German sun-worshippers bathing on the rocks, the broken crock smile of Wilder. It was the older Wilder—the one I imagined leading a quiet life on the other side of the world. I recognised the cut and thrust pattern in the corners of his eyes, torn between watching the tip of his rod for bites, and scanning the horizon for nosy reporters and writers.

The night before Clark flew out he rang up for the synopsis. On the phone Clark sounded let down by my failure, so I admitted to having a photograph I had managed to dig up from the bottom of a suitcase. The photograph is a police mugshot of the young car converter.

Wilder's hair is slicked back. His face is drained of colour. You can smell the free school milk on him. I showed Clark this photograph and immediately wished I hadn't. He was a little taken aback, I think. I wondered if Wilder's unsophisticated looks placed him in the false bottom suitcase era of Clark's genre. And what would Al make of it?

But, back to that afternoon I first saw Wilder on the rocks in a pair of old black stubbies. A Hawaiian shirt was open at the buttons. He didn't appear to have any other possessions.

The next time I looked I found Wilder trying to win over my children with a simple finger-play. 'Here's the church. Here's the steeple . . .'

My boys didn't take to him. They stood back warily. I didn't know whether it was relief or shame I should feel and, had Clark been here, whether I would have made the introduction.

The next night Wilder turned up in a bar along the esplanade of the old town. He had changed from his stubbies into some dreadful stovepipe black attire, otherwise he was the same. Clean-shaven for the evening. He sat at the far end of the bar. Detached, of course. I watched him in the mirror behind the bar. Every so often he looked over his shoulder; his grin unable to mask his ill ease.

Following his first prison escape, the newspapers describe a person happier to lounge outside the doors of a dance hall than risk inside, under the gaudy crêpe paper, the sweaty lights falling on his 'sallow complexion, fair hair, grey eyes and boil under his left eye'.

During the week Clark was away I ran into Wilder all over town. Where didn't he turn up?

The local tabac was no surprise. It offered a noisy scrabble of drinkers, and was largely patronised by the boat mechanics from the marina. Wilder leant up against the bar with a pastis and a leery grin. He chatted with a surly mechanic who had fixed the suspension on my car. Wilder looked happier, and I suppose some of that had to do with finding his name and the mechanic's teamed up on the chalkboard for the pool table.

Evidently Wilder favoured the same fruit stand in the market. He made a big thing of inspecting the fruit he chose. But his French was appalling. Often he was so slow getting the words out that the proprietor's eye skipped on to another customer. No loss there. Wilder only bought one piece of fruit at a time. He would take it over the road to the beach, where he sat on the flat white stones, among the mattresses and bare flesh.

The other night Clark rang from New York—breathless and shoulder-slapping, even over the phone. Al liked the Wilder script. But, and here a well-controlled note of caution came over the line, 'Al wants to relocate Wilder. He feels, you know, what with the market where it is, Wilder would be better off in Texas. They got long roads for car chases. Small towns. They talk a kind of English. Al had in mind a prison farm. He drove past it one time outside El Paso. These are just ideas you understand.'

'No, Clark,' I said. 'The answer is an unequivocal no.'

Then Clark did a typically North American thing. He apologised.

A postcard arrived within the week. It was of the Russian Tea Room. A contrite tone, with a PS. He had got more money from Al.

Meanwhile, mornings vanish one after another. I imagine Wilder standing alone on a farm staring out to sea, and listening to the wind.

Visitors and well-wishers climb over the wrought-iron fence. There's no keeping them out. They knock on the door and wait. Patiently they knock again. 'Just wondered if someone was there?'

The other morning a stately Maori woman with a large greenstone pendant gave me a fright. She called through the window just as I happened to be writing a scene about Wilder—about what?—well, it doesn't matter. Would I mind if her husband photographed us together? She thought against the walls of Mansfield's Isola Bella would be appropriate.

'Is that right?'

Is it?

Distance does not prevent one being implicated. Look at Clark and Capote in the Russian Tea Room.

Then this evening, from Beijing, a student's crumpled face stared from the pages of the *Herald-Tribune*. Picked out of the crowd. A random shot. His buckled trousers happened to match those of a 'counter-revolutionary scoundrel'. In the same newspaper, Rosemary Melo Nascimento—who launched a signal flare onto the field during a soccer match between Brazil and Chile—is to appear nude in next month's Brazilian edition of *Playboy*.

In a newspaper I first found Wilder.

I have become seriously worried about Clark. I wonder if he is writing about me. I wonder how a casual knock on my door has led to this unsympathetic portrait. It worries me to think what Clark will have to say of a man who goes rock climbing. And who otherwise spends all his time writing in a white-washed room about characters he will not talk about or admit into the light of day.

MICHAEL JACKSON

Michael Jackson (b.1940) was born and raised in New Zealand, but has lived in Sierra Leone, England, France, Australia and the United States, where he presently teaches anthropology at Indiana University. His work includes four volumes of poetry and two novels, of which one, Rainshadow, *was written while in Menton. He has won the Commonwealth Poetry Prize in 1976 and the New Zealand Book Award for Poetry in 1981. The following extract is taken from the unpublished novel* Pieces of Music: A Postmodern Picaresque.

There Go I

I wrote my first novel in the South of France. Like my sojourn itself, the novel ended abruptly, and for a long time I wanted to go back to Menton and bring to a close what I felt I'd left unfinished.

On the last page of the novel I describe a local clochard. Our paths crossed every day. We never exchanged a word, but I regarded him as a familiar and got to know his habits and beat by heart.

His hair and beard were grizzled and unkempt, his skin grimy and weather-beaten. Winter and summer he wore the same buttonless, stained overcoat, frayed trousers and plastic sandals. If he was a wild man, then Menton was his cage. All day he shambled along the seafront boulevard between Cap Martin and the Italian border, pushing a supermarket trolley full of rags and scraps of cardboard. He talked relentlessly to himself, berating the pavement, gesturing irritably. Mostly his eyes were averted, but if he happened to meet your gaze he would look straight through you. I thought of him as the Ancient Mariner and wondered what awful events weighed upon his mind. I imagined myself the wedding guest to whom he would one day unburden himself, and sometimes I dogged his steps, going far out of my way, in the hope that eavesdropping might give me access to his story. But either he spoke in patois or was mad, and in the end I had to piece together his story from hearsay.

According to Madame Picard, my *concierge*, he had been a mathematics teacher. He'd taught at the Lycée Mauriac. She hadn't the faintest idea how he'd become a drifter. 'You should ask your friend Giraldi,' she said, 'he'll know.'

Raoul Giraldi had grown up in Menton. His parents owned a small farm on the slopes above Castellar. Raoul once took me there, an exhausting climb along old mule tracks to a plateau high above the sea. Each time we stopped to catch our breath, we glanced back at

Menton and its littoral huddled far below. Above us loomed the eroded limestone bluffs of Ormea.

It was noon when we reached the place—a wilderness of broom and juniper. We sat in the shade of a stone pine and Raoul uncorked a bottle of Gigondas. I carved slices of country bread, spreading them with pâté and sharing out handfuls of black olives. Apart from the shrilling of cicadas, the landscape was silent.

Raoul wanted to know about my book. He said that if I was stumped for something to write about I could always turn to him. He had stories to tell which would set the Seine on fire.

When we had eaten, Raoul showed me the ruins of the house his great-grandfather had built. The roof had collapsed long ago, and an enormous fig tree was growing through the broken masonry.

Raoul regretted having let his birthright go to rack and ruin, and kicked at the crumbling terrace in disgust.

'It isn't only places that fall apart,' I said. And I mentioned the clochard who pushed the supermarket trolley up and down the seafront boulevard all day and each night slept shrouded in his filthy overcoat, outside the bureau de change at Garavan.

Raoul turned his head from side to side, as if trying to pick up the sound of something drowned by the noise of the cicadas. Yes, he said, he knew the clochard, but not by name. It was true he had been a maths teacher. His wife had been killed in a car crash. He had been driving. The accident had happened on the same corniche where Princess Grace met her death.

'What else?' I asked.

'It must have unhinged his mind, his wife dying like that. He went back teaching for a while, then one morning, in the middle of a lesson, he walked out of the classroom and never went back.' I wanted to know what language he spoke, whether it was French or Mentonnais.

'I don't know,' Raoul said, 'I've never spoken to him.'

I pressed Raoul to tell me more, but he knew no more. So I had to imagine him, this nameless man, after the death of his wife, convinced that nothing added up to anything in this world, that all our purposes are illusory, and that the sole solution to a problem from which the key integer has been lost is to subtract the other cipher, reducing everything to nothingness. I imagined him pining for a life more perfect for the suddenness of its ending, then craving annihilation, nullifying the arbitrariness of her death by contriving to bring about his own. I imagined him haunted by the hideous stillness of her face, by the conviction he had caused her death. For several weeks he refuses all contact with the outside world. He reads and rereads letters she wrote when he was in Senégal during the war. At night he opens her wardrobe and presses his face into her clothes, inhaling her presence. Friends prevail upon him to rejoin their backgammon circle in a neighbourhood café called Le Narval. He sits listlessly watching the counters move around the board, contemptuous of the significance his friends attach to the outcome of the game. A piece of popular music on the juke box overwhelms him with some unbearable memory and he shoves back his chair and stumbles into the street. He tries to drown his grief with pernod. He is visited by colleagues from the lycée who offer him consolation, assuring him that life goes on, that time heals all wounds. But he has seen into the void and knows this wound will never heal. Like Lot's wife he has been turned into a pillar of salt. He cannot rejoin the herd.

A few weeks pass and he is persuaded to return to the lycée. Everyone is full of sympathy and concern. He feels he deserves none of it. Colleagues address him warily and respectfully, as if the slightest harshness will make him fall apart. He shows no gratitude.

It is then that the gossip begins. In the playground and outside the school-gates, students relay what they have overheard at home. It is said he was drunk at the wheel of the car the day his wife was killed. In the opinion of some, he should have been charged with manslaughter. It is whispered that he visits the cemetery at night and sleeps on his wife's grave. He begins to take a perverse delight in his growing isolation, though sometimes he experiences himself as a mere shadow and is terrified. At night he wakes in a cold sweat. He hears the Paris-Milan *rapide* thundering through the darkness. He thinks of all the places he might go. There is nowhere. Now he listens to his own heartbeat, waiting for it to falter. But it is like the clock ticking on the table beside his bed, or the *rapide* vanishing into the night, something with a life of its own, timetabled and ineluctable.

He walks through the deserted streets of the old town and along the seafront, muttering under his breath, whimpering with grief. He contemplates the darkness of the ocean, its hiss and glut upon the shingles. One night he strips naked and swims straight out to sea, but when he tries to swallow water and sink into the depths he finds he cannot drown.

At the lycée, the absolute and unconditional truths of mathematics oppress him. One and one no longer equal two, since he is alive and she is not. One day, while he is writing equations on the blackboard, two girls start talking behind his back. He turns and stares at them. Again he experiences himself as a mere shadow. He rubs his hand across his chest and stomach to confirm his own substantiality. He opens his mouth to tell the girls to shut up, but his voice is parched and feeble. The girls look at him, taunting him to speak, demanding his anger, but the words stick in his throat. Now everyone is watching him struggling to get the words out. He walks toward the door in a daze, telling himself he is thirsty and needs water. A sinister murmuring follows him from the room.

In the street, the sunlight blinds him. He slumps onto a bench in the shade of a great plane tree. Cars pass up and down the road. Tourists are sitting under parasols in the harbourside cafés. Life is going on as usual, yet he is pervaded by a maddening numbness, so that the sound of traffic is dulled and he can hardly bear to look at the light glinting on the sea.

Half an hour passes. The Principal is standing over him, imploring him to speak. When his appeals fall on deaf ears and the maths teacher clasps his head in his hands, the Principal asks if he should telephone a doctor. You have been under a lot of strain, he says, and the clamour of the classroom doesn't make things any easier. Maybe you shouldn't have returned to teaching so soon. The Principal asks if he can drive the maths teacher to the hospital. Perhaps he could be given something to alleviate his distress.

The maths teacher tells the Principal to bugger off and leave him alone.

The Principal glances nervously up and down the street. 'But you can't just sit out here in the street! You might be recognised!'

The maths teacher assures the Principal that he knows what he is doing; he just needs to be alone for a while, there's nothing to worry about, he'll be all right. He won't be returning to the school though, not today, not next week, not ever. The Principal is no longer solicitous. He tells the maths teacher he has a school to run, other people to think about, responsibilities. He wants to hurl the word ingrate at him.

At first the maths teacher is hurt to find that the very people who went out of their way to help him when his wife died now spurn him. Colleagues at the lycée, whom he has dined with regularly for years, cross the street when they see him approaching—and this at a time when his clothes are still clean and decent, and he still bothers to wash and shave. But then it occurs to him that this ostracism is exactly what he wants. The only trouble is that he had wanted to repudiate *them*; it had not occurred to him that they would preempt his scheme, comply so readily with his wishes. It is then that he begins to let his beard and hair grow, to go for days without washing, to allow his clothes and shoes to fall apart, his body to fester. Now, when erstwhile colleagues see him in town, they disappear down side streets with dismay and repugnance on their faces. Now it is he who calls the tune, who drives them from him.

Gradually, his self-imposed exile comes to resemble madness. His debate with his own conscience is interminable. His thought never allows itself to become self-protective. Rather than using ideas and dreams to justify or forget the past, which is what so-called normal people do, he mercilessly keeps alive images of what has happened, torturing himself with regret, rehearsing endlessly the things he might have done or should have done to prevent his wife's death. Living vicariously, he lives another life. His absent-mindedness is literal. Oblivious to the present, because he discredits it as an illusion, he plunges back into the past like someone washed ashore from a shipwreck who realises that his beloved is drowning out at sea and risks his own life returning to save her.

A foul-smelling sack of a man, smoking butts he has picked up from the footpaths, punctuating his inner monologue with hopeless gestures, he crouches at night over his supermarket trolley in the entranceway of the bureau de change. He notices no one. He subsists on what he forages. Sometimes it is a day-old baguette from a boulangerie, smeared with mayonnaise. Sometimes it is a bowl of soup from the Sisters of Mercy. Sometimes it is a bottle of wine. He has no name, and because his identity is constructed so tortuously from events that others know nothing of, he is in effect a nobody, a *quelconque*, an idiot.

Consider now the audacity of the author of these pages. Beginning with some meagre autobiographical details, he constructs his fantasy. A clochard, with whom he has never exchanged a word, is given a past and a personality—the very things the poor drifter has done his utmost to render opaque. In good bourgeois style, the author has dragged the clochard off the streets, given him a bath, loaned him some of his own clothes, and found him a menial job in the factory where he himself is employed. The clochard has been made to pay for his marginality and mystery! The clochard craved anonymity; the author, refusing him that freedom, dresses him up and turns him into a walking parody of himself.

Countless adages caution us not to judge other people by ourselves, not to rehabilitate others in our own likeness. It is impossible, one is told, to know others as they know themselves. Yet we go ahead and grant ourselves all kinds of authorial privileges as if we were exempt from these discretionary rules. We gatecrash the private lives of others, presuming to enter into the consciousness of people whose language we do not speak, whose experiences we do not share, whose concerns are beyond our grasp.

Madame Ernaux was widowed at 55. She owned an apartment in the Riviera Palace—a hotel built at the turn of the century for royals and aristocrats. Victoria stayed there, and the Czar of Russia, who booked all the rooms on the upper floors so that no one but God would be above him.

Today, there is ugly red vinyl in the corridors. It makes a sickly squelching sound underfoot. At the top of the marble staircases, the friezes of pastel blue lilies and pink carnations are

Garden, Côte d'Azur
1991

decaying. Madame Ernaux's artificially-blonded hair has the shape of a beehive. Her eyebrows are pencilled lines, her cheeks savagely rouged. She speaks of the desolation of being alone. 'It is something you never get used to,' she says. 'And now this terrible tragedy of Grace's death.'

I had passed knots of people in the Avenue Verdun, watching the funeral on TV sets in shop windows. The newspapers were issuing colour supplements with banner headlines: Last Kiss Between Rainier and Grace.

'The newspapers are unforgiveable,' Madame Ernaux says. 'The way they probe and probe. Always looking for the truth. Things should be allowed to rest. What matter how the Princess died?'

My thoughts turn back to the clochard. What matter how his wife died? And then I think that though there are no good grounds for claiming certain knowledge of anything, there is every reason for trying to bridge the gap between ourselves and others. Life would be impossible otherwise, and thought would degenerate into mere solipsism.

Walking home alone the seafront, I am still thinking of the risk one runs in sharpening one's own ideas through dialogues, real or imagined, with others. In the process, others are eclipsed and their sense of who they are for themselves is lost. Perhaps this is why poets and so-called primitive peoples prefer to make stones, trees and natural phenomena their means of articulating human passions and ideas. Stones, trees and forked lightning do not, as a rule, talk back if they are misrepresented or maligned.

Perhaps my clochard wouldn't give a damn about knowing what I made of him, what tasks I set him to perform in the workhouse of my imagination. Perhaps if he read these pages he would recognise himself and be astounded that so much could be intuitively known. In any event, there is always a loss and a gain in any dialogue, and every writer has a need for his work to be redeemed by life. It is the vanity of authors to imagine that one day all the books ever written will be balanced by some daemon, and everything created in the minds of writers will match everything that has actually occurred in the world.

It had been raining. A fresh wind was blowing off the sea. A tricouleur snapped against a pole. Offshore, there was a slick of dirty water—froth, old corks, plastic containers, sticks and cigarette butts. And then the clochard was shambling toward me along the boulevard, trundling his supermarket trolley, upbraiding the sky with his index finger . . .

For years I have carried in my head these images of him, *mon semblable, mon frère*! At the centre of my imaginings is the idea of a man divided between two lives, just as individuals in traditional societies find themselves today divided between two worlds. So deep was the division in his life that one might speak of two incarnations—the life he led before the death of his wife and the life after. Often I find myself returning to those poignant lines of Joyce Johnson's, because they also belong to him . . .

'If time were like a passage of music, you could keep going back to it till you got it right.'

NIGEL COX

*Nigel Cox (b.1951) is a bookseller and novelist (*Waiting for Einstein, Dirty Work*) who was convening judge of the 25th Goodman Fielder Wattie Book Awards in 1992.*

When I Was a Writer

The Katherine Mansfield Room is a sort of above-ground cellar beneath the terrace of the Villa Isola Bella where Katherine lived for a few months in 1920-2. A photograph in Gillian Boddy's book about her shows her on the terrace but she was very ill at that time, scarcely mobile, according to the one handed down eye-witness report I've had of her, and I suspect she never descended to this spare room, this sleep-out—so was KM ever in the KM Room? But it's a good place to work; there's a sense that work is all that's ever been done within its thick creamy walls, which keep out France, and the sound of the trains, and the heat, even when it's not hot outside.

Inside it the Fellow tries to ignore the ghost (did Janet Frame sit facing this window or that one?) and get on with justifying the grant ($36,000, to cover travel, accommodation and living—Anne, Anneli and I will make it stretch 8½ months if we're careful).

This Fellow has a work chart to keep him honest; so far it's a five day week, from 8 in the morning till somewhere between 4.30 and 6p.m, with on average half an hour for lunch. There's no phone calls, no visitors, no interruptions, so you get on with it. I've never really had an extended stretch of being able to write all day before; it's tiring.

Every morning I come across town on the train, walk under the railbridge and, avoiding the dogs', which is everywhere, make the short climb up the av. Kathérine Mansfield to the Room. About a week ago I heard a hissing in the stone wall outside the gate to the Room's garden. A small pipe appeared to have sprung a leak within the wall, a dark trickle ran down the white of the 'ancient stones' and away along the gently sloping earth gutter. Your novelist, ever alert for a Real Story, followed the trickle ('This is your work!'), but became worried in case someone saw and thought him soft in the head.

For the next week when I turned up each morning, there was the trickle. After three days a clematis-like vine, enjoying the water, produced two bright yellow flowers. 'Voilà!' I said in my excellent French. Inside the Room I pressed on with the masterwork.

Then two days ago workmen arrived, six of them, from the Menton council, to clear the ground of any weeds, overhanging branches or rubbish. Everywhere in the city you can see the big clean-up in progress; August is coming and an immaculate Menton justifies the this-month-only inflation of prices. Menton (pop. 25,000) attends to presentation: the by-laws say you can paint your house any colour you like as long as it's terracotta. In my tiny garden the workmen remove all extraneous vegetable matter very efficiently, which I regret; urban France seems to be without backyards—our apartment has no 'outside'—and I rather like the little jungle at my back door. Then . . . and here's the question . . . did those workmen inform the water board there was a leak? Or is water usage in this town so carefully monitored that one of their dials told them they were losing precious drops? The latter isn't hard to imagine: this is a nation of dial-watchers, schedule-keepers and form-fillers, and France has had low rainfall for three years. The whole of Europe is short of water, I read, except (of course) England. Whatever: that afternoon the water-men arrived. I keep the gate to the Room's garden locked to deter the KM fans; I hurried out with the key. The workmen and I quickly established that we didn't have a language in common, and that I didn't know where the key to the stopcock on my end of the pipe was, and that I hadn't fiddled with it (honest!) and that, well, it was their business. This exchange had in it everything that a writer hates: failure in the language department, failure in the fixit department (okay, a male writer), a distraction from work that's not fascinating (let me rephrase that). They thrashed around in the bushes out there while I thrashed around in the bushes in here. Finally they shouted to me, 'Ay!' and the foreman asked with his hands, is there a telephone in there? 'No. Non.' He called me, 'Puta!' which I didn't go for all that much (though it's Spanish, isn't it? I searched for his mantilla), but I could see him thinking, That effete creature is worried I'm going to get my dirty boots all over his invaluable manuscript. I explained that there wasn't a phone—this is a writer's room—and then remembered for him that there's a cardphone at 'la gare'. He repeated the word, correcting my pronunciation, then off they went. They were back shortly with a huge spanner, which they took into the bushes—by then I was back to work and didn't watch—and departed. Later I discovered the Room's water had been cut off: no coffee, no toilet.

I waited a day, seeing if doing nothing would help, carefully recalling what had happened in minute detail. Away from home and without subtlety in the language of the country you're in, real encounters with the locals are rare, these microscopic incidents loom large.

I didn't want to start going to cafés for coffee, was quite soon peeing into very yellow toilet water. At lunchtime I assembled a letter, in French, for the General Secretary of the council here, M. Kettela, who is responsible for the Room; he speaks no English. I always write any complicated messages out and pass them to people to read (this is true even when I'm in New Zealand: writers trust writing) and it was fun getting the exact words for 'outside tap' and conjugating the verbs. Then, not wanting to be a bother, I decided I should try Direct Action first and checked all the man-holes and small access hatches, searching for the toby. Looking around the garden, I realised these hatches were everywhere, I found ten in as many square metres. They were slightly scary to open—I don't go much on big black spiders running up my bare arms, and I'm not sure if there's snakes around here. (At this point I remember that once, in Greece, needing a boulder to anchor a flysheet, I seized a hefty one and uncovered a nest of scorpions, one of them still on the boulder: squash!) The hatches gave access to beautifully maintained storm water pipes, all empty. There's something eerie about pipes that you can't see up: their hollow sound, the sense that any moment something might gush from them. These were part of such a complicated network. I thought about French organisation, which can be very impressive, and their determination to have things the way they want. To my relief the pipes had no occupants to face down, though when I opened the meterbox something rattled like a rat in behind its base-board. Then a large green lizard shot across the dials and

The Bakers of Arles
1990

disappeared behind the board again. I'm fond of lizards, they're always beautiful in colour, and I closed the door carefully. One day, checking the Room's mailbox (which I do obsessively about six times a day—so far it's yielded just one aerogramme), I found I'd squashed a tiny lizard, about an inch and a half long, faintly reminiscent of a tuatara, though this one, in death, was pale grey. It'd crawled in through the mail slot and then got caught in the hinge when I closed the box. These little everyday tragedies can make you feel desperate when you're away; there's no familiar for them to be absorbed into. It was another lizard that helped me feel at home here. This was a month ago, on the first really sunny day. The colours all changed and became soft, everything looked warm and sleepy in the steady light (Brian Boyd—Nabokov lived here—says, 'orangy-palmy-blue Menton', which gives the feeling exactly) and as I came under the railway bridge something rattled in the stone wall. I stopped, waited, and a beautiful lizard slowly extruded itself from a hole the power board had drilled to run cable into. It came out into the sun, blackgreen, with hidden lights among the stickles on its back and the red of toadstools on the undersides of its footpads. I felt at home because after that the lizard was something I looked for every morning. Fauna that's exotic (to you) seems to tell you you're in another country. I mean, all these French people could fly south, settle in New Zealand and learn to eat our lumpen food, but animals, reptiles especially, don't become ubiquitous easily.

Because I can't speak the language I seem to be paying great attention in this country to the natural world. But it frustrates me; there seems no way to identify the birds whose calls I hear outside as I work—so how will I write about them?

Late that afternoon I visited the Mairie, which is the mayor's nest, the Town Hall, armed with my carefully compiled letter. In Menton the Mairie is a beautiful building, formal, modest in its dignity (terracotta, of course), with a huge, clean tricolour, and tall, highly polished wooden doors. It houses the council offices, and the local Salle de Mariage, in which you must, if you wed in France, be married. This particular Salle was designed by Jean Cocteau in 1957; it's hard to imagine anything like it being allowed in New Zealand. The chamber itself is not vast but the symbolic figures Cocteau painted on the walls and ceiling are too big for the space, so that you seem to cower beneath them: prancing outlines, pale green, ochre, faintly erotic, their stylised perfection mocking the everyday creatures who are marrying beneath them. Under your feet the carpet is royal red, spread with imitation leopard skins. A thin light rises from black, diamond-shaped shades held at head-height by metal vines which climb, writhing, from the floor . . .

I'd been to the Mairie a few times and now approached it with caution as no one there apart from the Mayor speaks any English. (Everyone everywhere else speaks some English, whatever they tell you. My French, which I always try, is so bad that as soon as they hear it they reply in English. Of course, I'm in French mode and can't switch . . .) But I had my communication all written out: 'je suis Nigel Cox, je voudrais . . .' The counter-jumper sends me to wait by the coffee machine. Employees buy drinks from this machine every moment or two; they all talk to it. France is a highly automated country: at the station you can buy your train ticket, or something to eat, or drink, or sweets, from similar machines; or reserve a sleeper for Paris, or buy an airline ticket for anywhere in Europe, or have 50 business cards printed, or make photocopies, or do your banking—all without having to deal with a person you will have to be civil to. On the motorway the toll machine sorts the coins you toss into its wire basket and instantly returns you the correct change. The machines have personality: my train ticket automaton often says to me, 'Je suis hors service.' The telephone directory comes via a little TV called a Mini-Tel, which I can't work very well, despite the English language instructions. It can deliver just about anything, horoscopes, stock-market reports, the contents of department stores, flight information, but I keep getting a list of French provinces, which one do you desire? Other people play sex games on them—a guy down the road ran up a $20,000 phone bill.

M. Kettela (still at his desk most days at 6.30) waves me into his office, reads my communication, rings Works without having to look up the number. None of this, 'It's late, they'll be closed,' or, 'It's not my department,' which of course it isn't. One further call, he's got the right man. 'Ah—merci bien.' Then he explains all, very fast so I haven't got a clue what he's saying. But I can guess from his face: they're checking it out, I'm to come back in twenty minutes. 'D'accord,' I say, 'd'accord. A bientôt.' See, fluent.

The 'old town' of Menton is twelfth century and very beautiful: long cool dark streets, high sided, like slots, wind up towards the flying bell tower of the campanile. Up, up, that's where you look, to the pale scrollwork and the frescoes fading back into the sand-coloured façades, but down, down, that's where the drinks are, so I head down to the pedestrian precinct where you are reminded that 'café' is a French word. I have calculated that if everyone in this town wanted a restaurant seat at the same time it wouldn't be a problem. These restaurant-cafés are what the French do best. The service is casual, off-hand—but deceptively attentive, and of course the offerings are so wonderfully tasty. I have a bière while many people all better dressed and looking than I am stroll past in what seems to me to be terrific style. I could watch the people here forever—and they wouldn't care . . .

Upon my return M. Kettela seems to have done the trick. He talks absolutely flat out and he's probably high IQ too, I can hardly catch a thing. But I gather from his manner that he's finished with me, and I've made out 'demain', tomorrow, and he looks pleased with himself, so I go home.

Next morning when I arrive at 7.58 a.m. I see everything's been dealt to. The earth is open, the vine has been ripped out and is lying like a length of old twine. Within my little kingdom, water is again flowing as it should (remember 'Clochemerle', remember Pagnol) and I am content. At 8.30 the foreman turns up, we shake hands, we peer at the earth and nod seriously, stroking our chins. Two other officials turn up to make sure that all impediments to the writing of fiction have been removed.

Which they have. It wasn't a big job, but all of it was done after-hours, very swiftly, for a foreigner who doesn't speak French. I hope we could match this performance at home . . .

A bientôt, New Zealand.

Menton, late April 1991

That was when I was a writer. Now I'm back to being a bookseller who writes for three hours each morning—which seems another state entirely. But why? Maurice Gee, the 1992 KM Fellow, and a writer if ever there was one, tells me he only writes for three hours each morning, then he's 'finished, had it'—so is the difference in what you do for the rest of the day? In France I found the hardest thing was that, deprived of my usual distractions, I couldn't find a way to get out of my work overnight so I could come back to it fresh next morning.

So real writers stay in their writing all the time, is that it?

I did have spells of full-time writing when I was younger, patches where I was out of work or on holiday, but that was in the future-hungry days before I'd had anything published. Being the KM Fellow means that everybody you meet sees you as a writer, which is a role I find impossible to fill. In my mind writers are mythological, giants like Cocteau's Salle de Mariage figures; it's a company I aspire to.

But it was fun pretending; and I got an enormous amount of work done.

Try as I might I never felt at home in France. I did look every day for the lizard in the hole in the wall, but once I'd written this piece I never saw it again.

Auckland, January 1992

LOUIS JOHNSON

Louis Johnson (1924-1988) is a poet whose sixteen collections over a forty-year career include The Sun among the Ruins *and* Roughshod among the Lilies, *and latterly* True Confessions of the Last Cannibal: New Poems *and the posthumously published* Last Poems, *from which the two poems below are taken. Founder/editor of the New Zealand* Poetry Yearbook *(1951-1964), he lived in Australia for ten years before returning to New Zealand in 1980 as Writing Fellow at Victoria University. He became President of PEN (NZ) Centre and was awarded the OBE for services to literature in 1987 before dying in November 1988 in England, shortly after completing his tenure of the Katherine Mansfield Fellowship in Menton.*

Côte d'Azur

So many beautiful girls are wearing
the same face you'd swear they'd all bought masks
at a supermarket. I'm not complaining.

Beauty is beauty however processed
and regular. But when it becomes so uniform
something has got to give. Values diminish.

And I'm confused. I always knew there was
more to it than measurement, or that one year's
face would last a lifetime. Look at my own.

A walking, leering roadmap: and this morning
I limp along the waterfront on a cane from
falling downstairs to answer a late-night phone

and busting a leg on a radiator. But 1988
is the year the girls all look like peaches, their flesh
sweet and edible. They wear petulance

and a lisp as their trademarks. They parade

like fruit. I am glad to be old. I know if I must
choose again I'd do as badly as ever, and next

year, me and Miss Fourth-runner-up would be arguing
about who fooled who on a certain beach when
looking was free and all you had to decide was nothing.

16 June 1988

Trimming the Wick

(for the new Katherine Mansfield Menton Fellowship holder)

So many different things keep pouring in:
Europe unspooling like an endless scroll
past and present together along every road:

a castle atop each hill, mansions among
cumulous boughs and leaves: the sinous
grit of stone walls measuring hillsides:

canals and crowds and markets seething
just below eye-level: and the small streets
and lanes where the ordinary life sits down

to fries out of newspaper: hair-trigger squirrels
prayerfully eating and off like grease-spots
skidding on unseen alarms: you, trying to take it all

in with only six practical senses and a pen:
you know you are not equipped: you do
what you can with your slender means

tucking oddments, impressions, scents
and the smoke of battle into scraps of paper
packing them into your rucksack like frail eggs

to bear carefully back to the fellowship room
where the faith of others supports you
into believing you can make a little of much

Lara
1990

too much, and, maybe, even, persevere to a truth
if the Lady Luck should smile: and knowing
all the time a poetic truth is of the moment only.

It is for that moment you came here. Proud
perhaps: confident the sun shone for you
on such a morning while the swifts and swallows

swooped overhead with feathery messages. It is both
the ordinary and the miraculous that makes the effort
worth all the failing. Tomorrow you'll try again

and no doubt go home reduced in your purposes
somewhat more humble for having encountered
the muchness of much, the wastage of plenty

spilled from the horn of time you haven't got. Do not
be dismayed. Start again. Small. As you came.
You might feel a faint glimmer under the fingernail

like the seed of fire. Breathe gently upon it: focus
every atom of vision. Can you not hear now the faint
scratching of pens from each of the room's corners

where generations of all who've been plagued like you
with the itch to command words have spent lifetimes
trying to get it right and light the little lamp?

10 September 1988

MICHAEL GIFKINS

Michael Gifkins (b.1945) is an editor, critic and literary agent whose short story collections include After the Revolution and other stories, Summer is the Côte d'Azur *and* The Amphibians. *The latter volume is dedicated to Rosemary Hemmings, who died shortly before its publication in 1989.*

Dedication

You wake each morning bride to the day. A gossamer invitation, your nightgown sheens your body's hidden line. You pause before the mirror. You smile. You toss back glistening curls. Outside, light fingers damp tufts of mimosa, creeps in across the sill. Light in great lakes exerts its calm upon the sea. Along the Croisette, a general walks his dog. The general is stiff with great campaigns.

You dress your body. You are still smiling. At each fresh wave of memory the dog quivers, strains forward upon the leash at signposts from dogs before him. They stretch as far as the eye can see.

You are entering the Carlton, ice-cream cake of a grand hotel. It is night. All afternoon the people have waited for this moment. You imagine it is you they want to see. You are wearing your little black dress. Gendarmes with submachine guns line the steps. There are ropes to hold back the crowds. You clutch your ticket tighter still.

Offshore, the great white sharks gnaw lazily at their moorings. The moon beats a path to your empty room. Terrorists in velvet staterooms recite the Koran, fiddling with unsourced weaponry, declining offers of drinks. In a bath that seethes with Chanel a toe stabs at a gilded tap.

Up the stairs you go, unfazed by the crowds. Your escort is not handsome; you are a small group, from a country far away. You laugh, catching the attention of the paparazzi. You press yourself against him.

It is like being in a revolution. Outside the crowd is calling for the star of the festival, who is also your countryman and the reason you are here. They distort his name so that you believe they are chanting for an American car. When he returns he seems younger than a schoolboy. Women twice his age are trying to catch his eye. Fame makes his girlfriend distant from him by more than the twenty thousand kilometres he has journeyed. He prods gloomily at his escargots.

You are seated on the right hand of the festival director. You reply in a tongue that is not your own. Waiters bowl round like hooped snakes, pausing occasionally to hiss obscenities in your ear. The director toys with bread like a child, teasing it out into shreds.

You would like to help him, tell him that art is long and life has a habit of being short. But he is replaying his much-publicised argument with the internationally acclaimed actor . . . words were shouted in four languages in the lobby of the hotel. The actor publicly denounced the festival, left his honour behind him like a bad smell. It is said openly now, what they only dared whisper before.

The actor's face is the mask of death.

I am here on business, in the perennial search for funds. You hear of this eventually, though it is not the reason that we meet. This is at one of the many cocktail parties, where the champagne goes on and on. You glow from inside, like the Church of St-Michel; your eyes transmit a wonder which up close becomes a laugh. *Oh where do you go to, my lovely . . .?* the old tune asks.

'I'm from New Zealand,' you announce when we are finally introduced. The way you say it is both challenge and apology, why I can't be sure. Only later do I tell you that I know your country well from books.

We dance all night with your friends and then promenade to greet the dawn. I escort you back to your small hotel. In a side-street tabac we have coffee; there are glistening bikes parked outside. The black tee-shirts and red scarves of their riders are your adrenalin to start the day.

'I can say,' you remember, 'that I was kissed by a handsome man at dawn.'

We are walking under palm trees and night scents hang heavy in the air. I take a spray of jasmine and twine it through your hair. You are damp on your skin from dancing, and cold now to the touch. I kiss you as I might kiss a sister, not someone recently met.

Today I meet my backers, in a walled garden in Cap Martin—it is as familiar to me as loving, this slow seduction of money from its vaults. On impulse I suggest your presence. I hold my hands upturned, in supplication, above their wondrous marble table with its exotic food and drink. (This is a gesture I have learned from someone else.) They are a cagey pair, the banker and his mistress, indulging in some private fantasy that I must endorse without further question.

'But she is so *spectacular*!' Mme de Ferrier refers to you as though you were not there. 'And to think, all this way from New Zealand! *La Mansfield* would necessarily have been quite, quite jealous.' One day she will phone me transatlantic to discuss the character of Virginia Woolf.

I acquiesce with suitable deference to their quite unreasonable demands. They discuss their favourite stories, speaking as the characters would themselves. It is early evening when they ask the manservant to bring a pen.

You feel tired now; you are starting to wilt. You are pleased with the way things are.

The agreement is signed over cognac, so old that Fritz could well be serving ghosts. We are gathered like a family in the lengthening shadow of the land-based wall. '*They would never be alone together again,*' Mme de Ferrier proposes the toast that binds us all.

I suggest we go to the Casino but our host declines: the prospect of money in his hands has lost its power to amuse him. He warns us—without irony, I think—the extent to which commerce can be inimical to art. You ask that I take you to the villa where Katherine Mansfield tried to arrest her slow decline. You feel in your bones that I need all the assistance you can give.

It is a small building, quite unspectacular compared with some of the finer residences in Garavan. Upstairs there is darkness, but a dim light burns in the ground floor room which is

The Blue Garden
1991

now a memorial to the writer. It is a poet from New Zealand, on the fellowship which bears the writer's name. You are embarrassed. Quite irrationally (because you know her), you suddenly change your mind. You wait nervously as I try to frame the villa for the film. There is no way I can make of it any more than it is.

You turn to me and hold me fiercely, pressing me to your chest. Your feeling is that you are awkward, heroic. We stand like this for a long moment and you ask me how it will end. You have no idea of my patience. You quiver with light and clangour. Your world is suddenly awry. It is the express from Ventimiglia, bursting through the cushion of the night.

You are motoring through the region of the Loire to your assignation in the south. The small Citroën you pick up the day before from the tourist scheme in the Champs de Mars. You are protected by Autostop: a newer car should this new car break down; accommodation, transport, insurance. They try to sell you extras which they present with Gallic flair—wheel kits, foglights, everything that les madames would want to cause their journey to be more *confortable*. You do not say anything. You are driven, both of you giggling, to the bowels of a huge parking building in a district you do not understand. For your benefit and your education the chauffeur takes unnecessary risks. There is your little car. A mechanic tells you what to do in all of fifteen seconds. You emerge into rush-hour traffic. You stop, you start. You try to remember your left side from your right. You are behind a big camion. It seems that all Paris is burning. Your car is filled with smoke. It is an early summer. You phone Autostop.

'It is regrettable.'

They have neglected to put the oil in the car.

The second car is dark red, the colour of your blood. Parked outside this smallest chateau, it reminds you now of London. It is the off-season. You make an appointment with the concierge by phone. He gets up. He dresses. He breakfasts. He takes his time. You press every bell at every entrance to the castle.

Eventually it emerges from a high gothic window, this severely correct French student head. He recalls for you a Truffaut movie, along with everything else in France. *Dix minutes*. Deer as a courtly sideline graze the boundary fence. You inspect the crypt while you wait. You suddenly feel cold. Maxine is asking you about AIDS. She thinks you are far more likely to get it from blood, in spite of the precautions. She carries twelve dozen of her own precautions and you comment on her dedicated optimism. She is your best friend, having recently lost her father. In your purse are the three Durex you keep as a talisman; it would be foolish, coming this far, to undergo a merely topical demise.

Inside the chateau is history, fast forward with no concessions. In whispers you translate. You are a party of tourists. There are two of you. There can be no deviation from history as it is laid down. It takes forty minutes, twenty lifetimes. You tip the student twenty francs.

At the crossroads back from the chateau there is a typical country café. The owners seem retarded and you notice tinned peas upon a shelf. You ask for espresso, anything. There are small vacuum flasks on the counter. To your consternation these contain the coffee. They pour you lukewarm cups of tar.

Maxine does the driving; she says she feels it is her duty and you do not have the energy to object. On the autoroute you colonise the slow lane as fuel-injected Europe slips past at 200 kilometres an hour. 'Better to travel safely than to arrive dead on time.' Your best friend winces as you laugh.

Your son has difficulty walking. It is a mild condition which may in later life provide the basis for reflection upon the norm. Your daughter, on the other hand, is quite healthy. Recently she has acquired the habit of rubbing her body slowly against your startled male friends. You could, if you wish, read whole novels in their eyes. You do not want to warn her.

A friend of your ex-lover's phones to tell you that he (your lover) collects only exceptional women. (She imagines this will please you.) Currently there is an involvement with an archaeologist, which explains why he did not meet your plane. The archaeologist is a young Frenchwoman of great vivacity and piercing intelligence who is making her contribution to a post-modern understanding of Pharaonic ritual. You picture them both quite easily beneath a nightmare weight of stone. You are pleased for your ex-lover, that he is sharing the passion which leads her to the burial chamber. His own special project is an exploration of the infrastructure of the aesthetic impulse of what remains of the Western world. You consider this as you spend the whole day in a London hospital. You are fascinated by the soft bubbling of your own and another's blood.

The coffee is so bitter that you need to cleanse yourself with wine.

We are walking the seacoast from Monaco in the direction of Cap Martin. A drugged-out Princess Stephanie enters an exclusive private hospital. Her press release claims stress caused through overworking. A famous actress leaves the road at 140 kilometres an hour. Each day twenty kilograms of letters bear her the country's undying affection. Distinguished surgeons contemplate the reconstruction of the muscles of her face. On front pages her Porsche lies crumpled. The advertisement beside it is for Veuve Clicquot champagne.

You imagine that our picnic will make you homesick. When I ask you why, you cannot say.

We are jammed amongst the rocks which tumble on the seafront of the great estates. Through the tropical profusion of walled gardens their towers are glimpsed against the sky. A fisherman (you call him *piscator*) is busy down beneath us. The weather is unseasonal, but he is dressed in suit and tie. You say that it is the ghost of Italo Calvino.

The ants are feasting on crumbs of *pain complet*. You demand that I pass my glass. It was the horror of her own insignificance, you claim, that caused Katherine Mansfield's death. You wave your hand about you, encompassing the scene. The fisherman, I mention, might be delighted to see you bathe.

Your son was born with a massive tumour; it was pressing on his brain. Though the terminology surprised you, the experts pronounced it to be benign. You watched as he emerged from that first operation, a tiny parcel swaddled like a corpse. Every year as he grew bigger, they replaced the device inside his head.

I disagree with you about Mansfield; we discuss the psychopathology of health. Your son slept in a cot beside you, so you could feed him in the night. Pursing tiny lips, he would take your warm and heavy breast. You talked to him as he suckled, asking him if he was ready yet to swap. You smile fondly at this memory: his first words were 'other side!'

Each evening I review my plans; the shape of the film to come. There will be love interest, though my treatment of Murry is bound to attract comment. Perhaps the purists would prefer him cast in a traditionally demeaning role? There will be the self-confidence of a major talent abroad, sustained by backward glances at a sun-filled antipodean childhood; there will be the recognition of the pain of loss, the intimations of mortality. But above all, there will be the gathering dark.

You move your face above me, as if to shield me from the glare. I blink to adjust my vision to the sudden change of light. The cascade of curls frames the perfect oval of your face. The sheen of your teeth is like a string of pearls.

When we awake, both sun and fisherman are gone. You feel that perhaps your mood should change. In a small café you drink glass after glass of pernod, watch the water cloud the clear spirit. You intimidate the waiter with an hauteur I had not imagined before, calling for olives, for a clean glass. You organise where we should dine. You even comment on the style of my shirt.

Your head is telling you one thing; it is a refrain of which you are endlessly aware. You heart tells you something quite different and you feel yourself betrayed.

In 1888 Katherine Mansfield is born in Wellington, New Zealand. At the age of fifteen she attends Queen's College, London. No doubt her father wishes her 'finished' in the manner of the time. In 1948 your mother comes to New Zealand, a woman of courage and sophistication, a devotee of Europe. Your father she meets in London, a New Zealand soldier convalescing from the war. They settle in the King Country, at a place so small its name is omitted from the road maps. Your mother likes the sound of 'the King Country', but soon finds that it is filled with dog bones and old wire.

She sends to Harrods for clothes to dress you, and your sisters when they come. You remember especially a white, large-wheeled pram. In high heels and stockings, she walks the pram across the farm. There are photographs to prove this. Look at you! Three little girls dressed all in white! There is lace, there are bows. There are little white socks. What will the kids think of you at school?

Your father is tall, a handsome man and rangy. All day the rams are tupping the ewes, despite the bidibids in their wool. On sale days your father roams the district, visiting other farmers' wives. The men wear oilskins and roll their own tobacco, are hoarse-voiced over bargains. In their absence your father is offered many cups of tea.

You marry a man who is taller and more handsome than your father. You don't know what else to do. During the birth of your son, your husband shouts at you for suffering. It is typical, he says, that you should make such a fuss about a little pain. When he marries a second time he calls his new son by the same name as your first. He cannot identify with imperfection; with this small, imperfect child. You tell your husband but he will not discuss it. You find out later that he is having an affair. The doctor states it will have to go, that they will have to remove your breast.

The poet says she knows you when I interview her for the film. You sell the furniture and fly to California for a cure. This is ten years ago. Even then you like to travel. You discover that there are not enough apricot kernels in the whole wide world. The poet shows me passages in Katherine Mansfield's diaries, speaks of the 'great honesty' of her soul. Her poems are small domestic tragedies and she can write one every hour.

Today I prepare myself for the arrival of my new director, who is an upright man, and proud. I ask you to be his assistant because I can see you need the job. All morning I work on the scene of Katherine at Isola Bella: the writer is composing letters home; mimosa is heavy outside the casement and her room is full of light.

Over coffee we discuss your illness. There is a tumour in your chest that you insist on retaining to monitor the status of your disease. Throughout the history of your condition you witness tumours come and go. You are an international courier. The blood they give you in London is the blood that circulates in France.

Mme de Ferrier telephones and asks the three of us to lunch. You decide you do not like the banker, but accept charity for art.

You pause before the mirror but the mirror lets you pass. You are wearing your small black dress. You smile. You toss back glistening curls. The Mediterranean proceeds to Africa. Mimosa is close outside the window and light reflects its calm back to the world.

List of Paintings

Acknowledgements

For permission to reproduce the material in this anthology acknowledgement is gratefully made to the publishers and copyright holders of the following: 'A Patriot Abroad' from *Being Pakeha* by Michael King, Hodder & Stoughton (NZ) Ltd; '123 Rue Longue' by Margaret Scott, published by permission of the author; 'Buying a Car' from 'The Town' in *Five for the Symbol* by C.K. Stead (Longman Paul Ltd), published by permission of the author; *Trouble Spots* (extract) by Owen Leeming, published by permission of the author; 'Do Not Touch the Exhibits' and 'Gare SNCF Garavan' from *The Loop in Lone Kauri Road: poems 1983-1985* by Allen Curnow (AUP/OUP), published by permission of the author; *Faith of Our Fathers* (extract) by Spiro Zavos, University of Queensland Press, 1982; 'Not So Far From Godwit Bay' by James McNeish, published by permission of the author; 'Uncle On—and Off—His Bike', 'Uncle's Love Song' and 'Uncle Casts a Paper Dart' from *Uncle & Others* by Barry Mitcalfe (Coromandel Press/Caveman Press), published by permission of Jackie Mitcalfe; 'Gens et Sites' by Philip Temple, published by permission of the author; 'Interior Decorating' from *Giotto's Elephant* by Michael Harlow, John McIndoe Ltd; 'Menton Vignette I' (first published in *Te Ao Marama*, Reed Publishing (NZ) Ltd), 'Menton Vignette III' and 'Ozymandias Revisited' by Rowley Habib, published by permission of the author; 'In Katherine Mansfield's Shadow' by Russell Haley, published by permission of the author; *Living in the Maniototo* (extract) by Janet Frame (Braziller, New York), published by permission of Curtis Brown (Australia) Pty Ltd; *The Quick World* (extract) by Lauris Edmond (Bridget Williams Books), published by permission of the author; 'Gwen Walks the Dog' by Maurice Gee, published by permission of the author; 'chess', 'the poetry reading' and 'a woman amongst girls' by David Mitchell, published by permission of the author; 'All Those Daffodils' from *Explosions on the Sun* by Marilyn Duckworth (Hodder & Stoughton (NZ) Ltd), published by permission of the author; 'A Walk Along the Crocodile's Tail' by Witi Ihimaera, published by permission of the author; 'Moonflowers' by Lisa Greenwood, published by permission of the author; 'Me, Clark and Wilder' from *Swimming to Australia* by Lloyd Jones, published by permission of Victoria University Press and Michael Gifkins & Associates; 'There Go I' by Michael Jackson, published by permission of the author; 'When I Was a Writer' (first published in *Sport*) by Nigel Cox, published by permission of the author; 'Côte d'Azur' and 'Trimming the Wick' from *Last Poems* by Louis Johnson (Antipodes Press), published by permission of Cecilia Johnson; 'Dedication' from *The Amphibians* by Michael Gifkins, Penguin Books (NZ) Ltd.

Photo credits. *Helen McNeish*: Eze-village, p. 13; James McNeish, p. 8; Bandol, p. 5; Isola Bella, p. 8; tombstone, p. 7; terrasse at Isola Bella, p. 6; KM's landlady's grandson, p. 11; wicker chair, p. 3; *R. Judlin*: Owen Leeming, p. 1; David Mitchell, p. 7; *Michael King*: Corsica, p. 2; Patrick White, p. 4; *David Playne*: Menton from Garavan, p. 10; *Michael Gifkins*: self, p. 16; clochard, p. 15; Waterfield, p. 14.